"Shall we finish listing all the rules, Red?"

Like the brush of a feather, his lips came down on hers, soft and sure. "A kiss for company," he explained sardonically. "It will seem pretty damn odd if we don't, on occasion."

Suddenly, his lips descended again, with only slightly more pressure. A sudden, disquieting warmth was flooding her veins—as if she had just drunk a snifter of brandy.

"We'd better get all the rules out of the way, Red." His next kiss forced her lips helplessly apart. Like a series of shocks, she felt the thick, heavy texture of his hair in her fingers, the graze of his thighs against her own...

Dear Reader:

The event we've all been waiting for has finally arrived! The publishers of SECOND CHANCE AT LOVE are delighted to announce the arrival of TO HAVE AND TO HOLD. Here is the line of romances so many of you have been asking for. Here are the stories that take romance fiction into the thrilling new realm of married love.

TO HAVE AND TO HOLD is the first and only romance series that portrays the joys and heartaches of marriage. Its unique concept makes it significantly different from the other lines now available to you. It conforms to a standard of high quality set and maintained by SECOND CHANCE AT LOVE. And, of course, it offers all the compelling romance, exciting sensuality, and heartwarming entertainment you expect in your romance reading.

We think you'll love TO HAVE AND TO HOLD romances—and that you'll become the kind of loyal reader who is making SECOND CHANCE AT LOVE an ever-increasing success. Look for four TO HAVE AND TO HOLD romances in October and three each month thereafter, as well as six SECOND CHANCE AT LOVE romances each and every month. We hope you'll read and enjoy them all. And please keep your letters coming! Your opinion is of the utmost importance to us.

Warm wishes,

Ellen Edwards

Ellen Edwards
SECOND CHANCE AT LOVE
The Berkley Publishing Group
200 Madison Avenue
New York, N.Y. 10016

Second Chance at Love®

A DARING PROPOSITION
JEANNE GRANT

SECOND CHANCE AT LOVE
BOOK

A DARING PROPOSITION

First edition published October 1983

First printing

"Second Chance at Love" and the butterfly emblem are trademarks be-
longing to Jove Publications, Inc.

Printed in the United States of America

Second Chance at Love books are published by
The Berkley Publishing Group
200 Madison Avenue, New York, NY 10016

A DARING PROPOSITION

Chapter 1

A HOT, FAST wind blew off Lake Michigan, adding noise and dusty debris to the late August heat wave, as Leigh Sexton walked briskly along the sidewalks of downtown Chicago. Ahead, the skyscraper that housed the distinguished architectural firm of Hathaway, Hathorne, and Brent beckoned with the promise of air-conditioned comfort and insulation from the din of industry and rush-hour traffic.

Entering the cool, silent lobby of the building, Leigh felt instantaneous relief. But as she crossed the patterned carpet to the elevator, stepped in, and punched the button for the twentieth floor, a film of perspiration coated her brow. Leigh knew it had nothing to do with the humidity and smog she had just escaped, but reflected her own inner apprehensions.

For the last four weeks, Leigh had been coming regularly to Hathaway, Hathorne, and Brent to audit the firm's accounts, but now the job was over. Indeed, the cocktail party now taking place on the twentieth floor was a celebration of just that, and more specifically of the fact that Leigh's careful audit had saved the firm three-quarters of a million dollars. Ordinarily she would have pleaded flu rather than attend this type of bash. Though she was only twenty-five, Leigh preferred a reclusive private life to the social whirl most women her age enjoyed. In the three years she had worked as a CPA for White's Accounting Firm, she had consistently refused every social invitation that had come her way through job contacts, despite the protests of her gregarious boss, Jim White. It had not been Jim's insistence that she attend this party that had induced Leigh to make an exception for Hathaway, Hathorne, and Brent. No, it was simply that this was the last chance she might have to corner one particular man. Her decision to do so had been weeks in the making—years, really, she thought fleetingly. Yet it was the idea of that upcoming confrontation—the awkwardness and embarrassment of it—that had churned her emotions to their present state of turbulence, and caused beads of moisture to break out on her high, pale forehead.

The elevator came to an abrupt halt, and the doors opened. Leigh paused only a moment before stepping over the threshold and automatically brushing a hand across her temples to make sure her rich coppery hair was properly restrained. She could already hear laughter coming from the reception room where the party was being held. In the long floor-to-ceiling windows she caught a glimpse of her reflection. Clear wire rims blocked the beauty of her wide-spaced brown eyes and dimmed their amber glints; the high-collared brown linen dress was a loose smock that hid the voluptuous curves of her womanly figure. Only someone who looked closely would see the uniform for the disguise it was, and hardly anyone ever did look closely. Most people expected a certain sexlessness from a CPA, which was precisely why the job suited Leigh. She was reassured by her unprepossessing reflection in the glass.

Wending her way past mostly empty tables, she took a deep breath and joined the party. The closed area already reeked of alcohol and smoke; and although uniformed waitresses proffered trays of delicate-looking canapés, most people seemed to prefer liquid refreshment. Immediately, Leigh saw the burly form of her boss and heard his jovial laughter, which was aimed at Taylor Brent, one of the firm's partners and its marketing director.

Two dozen people crowded the room, none of them the man Leigh was looking for. A strolling bartender approached, and she accepted a martini that she had no intention of touching, then unobtrusively made her way to the window. The glass wall opened onto a view of Chicago's skyscrapers and Lake Michigan's serene dark waters. Leigh knew that the image she presented was as calm and remote as that of the lake; yet many layers beneath was a heart that wouldn't stop pounding and a deepening feeling of dread.

She turned, as if by instinct, the minute Brian Hathaway strode through the door. An irritated expression showed on his rugged features, and he was still sporting rolled-up shirt-sleeves: obviously, his secretary had just reminded him of the affair; and just as obviously, despite his incongruous reputation as both playboy and creative genius, he did not like mixing business with pleasure. By day he was seduced by his drawing board, but when the sun went down *he* did the seducing—in a different arena. One columnist had quoted him as cynically admitting there was no woman he didn't like, as long as she was pretty and prone.

Taylor Brent immediately approached him, as did Leigh's boss. Both men appeared anxious to soothe the wounded tiger, their conviviality loud and deliberate. Unlike the other guests, Brian took coffee, and he seemed to be looking for an excuse to get back to work, half-listening to Taylor and Jim, while his coal-black eyes restlessly surveyed the rest of the gathering.

Leigh felt her heart skip a beat as he took the time to acknowledge her with a small nod. There had been several occasions when she'd had to contact him directly because the other partners were absent. The first time he had made an automatic, raw head-to-toe assessment of her potential femininity before getting down to business. On the other occasions he'd been preoccupied, yet not lacking in either patience or even kindness, which surprised her because he had a reputation for neither. He could be a formidably unapproachable man, unless one had legitimate business and intended to waste none of his time. And Leigh hoped desperately that he would see the request she planned to make of him today in just that light.

As she approached the trio of men, she tried, unsuccessfully, to quell the fluttery sensations in her stomach. She sighed. She ought to know by now that fear didn't simply disappear by willing it away. She'd lived with the emotion for how long . . . eight years? Fear of men—and no matter how neutrally he'd treated her in the past, Brian Hathaway was definitely a man.

"If you don't mind, I've been trying to live down that damn article for over a month," she overheard Brian say curtly to her boss.

"Oh, come on," Jim White chaffed, "you must have at least gotten a good laugh out of it! My wife's been telling me that now all her friends are making out their own fantasy lists."

"You'd better watch it, Jim," Taylor Brent warned. "If Hathaway ever got his hands around that columnist's neck . . . For close to two years, she's apparently been taking on our resident bachelor-around-town as her own personal cause."

"I've never even met the damned woman," Brian growled. "Hell, I don't mind her chit-chat column. But that feature article . . ."

"It was only an attempt at levity," Jim protested.

"Babies are no subject for levity—not in my life," Brian snapped.

For a long moment, Leigh could not prevent herself from staring with total absorption at Brian Hathaway. He was a full six feet of lean angles and bone, power and assurance radiating from the strong set of jaw and shoulder. Beneath the harsh fluorescent lights, the strong planes of his face took on hollows, and with his burnished tan and piercing jet eyes it had a faintly Indian cast. Next to her extroverted boss, Brian Hathaway appeared to be an ominously quiet man, self-aware, confident, alert, warily intelligent—and distinctly male. And next to his all-American, clean-cut partner, *handsome* seemed a tame word to describe his appearance. *Sexual* was more applicable. *Stark, primitive, virile . . . leashed.* In Leigh, he evoked a powerful desire to simply cut and run. She took a small sip of the unwanted martini, welcoming whatever artificial courage the alcohol could supply.

The subject of their conversation... She had read and reread that Sunday feature section on fertility some weeks ago, and that was when her decision had jelled. At the end of a half-page article on artificial insemination, the columnist had described a clinic located in California, a sperm bank for Nobel Prize winners. Whimsically, the writer had made up her own list of local men whose genes should not be lost to mankind. Brian Hathaway had been at the head of that list. Obviously, the notable young architect was uncatchable as a husband, the columnist had pointed out, given the long string of leading socialites who had tried over the last decade. And so, not to waste those unbearably sexy looks and unequaled brilliance in the design field...

"She's got you labeled as one of her 'ideal men,'" Jim White unwisely continued to tease.

"Of all the absurd labels," Brian said contemptuously, and with a single glance that silenced Leigh's boss, he stepped aside.

For just that instant, he was alone, and Leigh could sense he did not intend to stay much longer. It was the moment she had been waiting for, but now that it was here she felt only a sick, thudding sensation in her stomach. Come on, Leigh, she urged herself desperately. Tentatively, she forced her feet to move forward before he reached the door. "Mr. Hathaway?" she inquired quietly.

He turned, adjusted his eyes down to her lower height, the irritation on his features quickly masked for her benefit.

"I wondered if I could possibly have a few minutes of your time?" she requested. "I... where we wouldn't be interrupted?"

A frown barely furrowed his forehead, a blend of curiosity and annoyance. "You're the lady who worked on our books, aren't you? You did us a good turn, Miss Sexton. I can spare you five minutes. My office is private."

She took a breath, following him silently to his inner sanctum, where teak paneling and a plush blue carpet created a feeling of serenity and privacy. His desk, of brilliantly polished walnut, was clear. In contrast, the drawing board in the corner was still uptilted; there was a tray on the floor with a half-eaten sandwich and a cup of cold coffee.

"There's no need for you to be nervous," he said with that special low-pitched timbre he had used on her before. "I can guess why you wish to speak with me, Miss Sexton."

She stared at him, totally taken back.

"You've left your mark here in the last four weeks," he complimented her graciously. "On the surface—you're a very quiet, reserved lady, but there must be more to you than that. No one else has ever taken on my comptroller, criticized his computer, and left him smiling. My secretary's been muttering under her breath about the hours you've put in, and I've spent enough time with you myself to know that you're a perfectionist in your work—a quality I admire in my employees. Our personnel director usually hires people in your area of expertise, but if you're looking for a position, I—"

Leigh shook her head almost wildly, appalled as she realized he was about to offer her a job. "I appreciate your offer, but I'm perfectly content at White's," she assured him with a faint tremor in her voice. Hearing the quaver, she struck it out determinedly with a skill she had developed over eight long years. "I . . . my request is of a terribly personal nature. It's difficult to—"

He interrupted her with a low chuckle of amusement. "Well, well, well," he said, his deep voice tinged with innuendo. "They do say still waters run deep, but I never imagined . . ." He let his voice trail suggestively as, with a swift gesture, he removed her glasses, put them on his desk, and then, taking out the hairpins that held her severe coiffure in place, gently shook her flaming tresses onto her shoulders. Paralyzed with astonishment and horror, Leigh saw his eyes trail downward as if his gaze could penetrate the smocklike dress to see the ripe curves that lay beneath, and linger on the shapely legs her sheer stockings left unconcealed.

"It's odd, but just this afternoon, when I saw you at the party, I had a premonition of the attractive woman who chooses to hide behind that ridiculous disguise. I suppose it's to keep off unwanted admirers? Really, Red"—his gaze

flicked over her gleaming copper-colored hair—"is it necessary to go to such lengths?"

"Mr. Hathaway—" She had no sooner found her voice
than he cut her off.

"Under the circumstances, you might call me Brian. Better yet..."

As his arms encircled her waist, drawing her to him, and
his full, sensual lips moved toward hers, Leigh knew a
moment of sheer panic. Conjuring up all her strength, she
wrenched herself from his grasp and moved away so that
the broad expanse of his desk stood between them.

"Mr. Hathaway," she said quickly, sharply, "you seem
to have misunderstood me. This is a business proposition..."

"Of a terribly personal nature?" He quirked an eyebrow
ironically as he watched her reach across the desk to scoop
up her glasses and hairpins. He waited until she had restored
the severe hairdo and readjusted the glasses before continuing. "Please excuse my *misunderstanding*," he said sardonically, folding his arms across his chest. "Your
words—"

"Yes, yes," she interrupted brusquely, feeling more in
control now that her armor was again secure. "My choice
of words was unfortunate, I admit that. There really is no
graceful way to ease into the subject, and I suppose I'd best
be blunt about it."

"Please." The eyes that met hers were granite-hard, yet
intrigued. "But you needn't cower behind my desk like a
frightened kitten, Miss Sexton. I'm not used to having women
flee my embrace as if I were a viper, and you can be sure
I won't lay a hand on you again."

"I'm sorry," she apologized stiffly, but stayed behind
the desk. Her back still seemed to burn with the imprint of
his fingers, and the scent of his warm, coffee-flavored breath
lingered in her nostrils. It had been the old fear of a man's
touch, a man's advances, and yet...

But Leigh refused to dwell on the unsettling sensations
Brian Hathaway's embrace had aroused in her. Instead, she
met his dark gaze and took a deep breath. "I want a child,"
she said quietly, but very clearly. "I will offer you ten

thousand dollars to impregnate me. Artificially," she added swiftly. "And of course anonymously. Your anonymity would be stipulated in the contract, and—"

"Hold it, Red." His hands suddenly dropped to his sides, fists clenched. "I've taken all I'm going to take on the subject of that article. If your boss talked you into this as some kind of practical joke—"

"I'm not joking, Mr. Hathaway. I read the article about fertility several times. And I've read some other newspaper articles about you. It's obvious that you don't think much of the home and family scene, that you're not interested in . . . personal commitments . . . which is fine, you see, with me. What I've read has led me to believe that the moral overtones involved in having a child this way wouldn't bother you."

He stared at her. "I think," he said grimly, "you'd better sit down."

At least he was taking her seriously now, but his reaction didn't seem promising. "There's really no reason to take up much more of your time," she said, and then, at his silence, added swiftly, "If the money isn't enough . . . I work because I like to work, Mr. Hathaway. I have money of my own; I could offer you more. And your anonymity is probably even more important to me than it is to you; you would have my word, and the contract would absolve you of any future financial, moral, or legal responsibility for the child—in fact, you wouldn't even have to see me beyond this single instance. If—"

"I need a minute to breathe, Red. Do you mind?" The caustic note stilled whatever urge she had to attempt any further persuasion. She could feel him considering in the silence that followed. A frown etched parallel lines on his forehead. "You're actually serious, aren't you?"

"Yes. If it's more money . . ."

"I don't need money, Red," he said tartly. "You should know that. You worked on the books." He stood straight, shoveling his hands into his pockets. When he spoke again, the sharpness in his voice was gone. Thoughtfully, he said, "I take it there's some medical reason you can only have a child this way?"

She swallowed.

"I . . . I . . ."

More gently, he probed, "Is it that you have a husband who can't have children? I don't see a ring on your finger."

She glanced down at her hands and then determinedly out the window.

He tried one more time. "You've drawn some very personal conclusions about me, Red. Perhaps I should feel flattered that you've chosen me to be the father of your child. But you seem at least partially motivated to do so because you think I could care less about a child of my own blood. Not very flattering. In fact, insulting," he said dryly, and then added more encouragingly, "I'm not asking for your life history or any personal details that might embarrass you. But there must be *some* reason—"

"Mr. Hathaway," Leigh broke in, "I'm in every way prepared to support a child, and if necessary I'm willing to prove that."

"That doesn't exactly answer my questions."

"No," she agreed, and added very softly, "I won't answer any questions. I'll pay you whatever you want and agree to whatever legal terms you think best, but . . . no questions."

She saw his jaw tighten. Clearly he wasn't used to a "no," either in his public or private life. Tentatively, she touched trembling, damp fingertips to her temples. She was losing the single chance she might ever have, and she was losing her poise at the same time. "Mr. Hathaway," she said desperately, "sometime there might be someone else I could ask. I don't think so. You see, the way the newspaper said you feel about marriage and family ties . . . it seemed perfect. Your lifestyle would be a guarantee for both of us that it wouldn't mean anything to you, just an hour in a doctor's office." From her purse she drew out a small slip of paper and slid it to the far edge of his desk. "My number's unlisted. Perhaps you would at least think about it, and if you should decide . . ."

He reached the door in long, easy strides before she possibly could. The potential was all there, suddenly, the intrinsic power of a man over a woman. The throbbing in her temples increased. She had known it was going to be worse with him because of the kind of man he was, but still she was unprepared for her reaction to his proximity: the

scent of him, so blatantly male; the hint of a shadow on his
chin; the hardness of his chest accented by the stretch of
shirt fabric across it; and their mutual consciousness of the
scene that had occurred only moments before, when he had
tried to kiss her and she had fled from his embrace. His
hand was on the doorknob. She was imprisoned until he
opened the door. The memory of David Hines suddenly
took shape next to him, like a ghost, not nearly so overtly
masculine, nor with the physical or intellectual sort of strength
inherent in this man. David was by far the lesser image . . . and that in itself made the blood drain from her face,
increased a hazy, dizzy sensation that the floor was tumbling
beneath her.

Lightning-fast, she felt him reaching out to support her
arm. His fingers seared the flesh of her shoulder, shocking
her brutally back to the present. Leigh jerked awkwardly
away with her palm protectively out in front of her. "I . . . thank
you. I'm sorry for the initial misunderstanding, sorry if I've
affronted you. You've been very kind." And she was gone,
before he had a chance to say a word.

Chapter 2

"IT'S ABOUT TIME you got home," Robert grumbled affectionately. In an Old World gesture of courtesy, the short white-haired man rose from his rocking chair when he saw Leigh coming through the kitchen doorway.

"I've been home nearly two hours," she replied, and gave him a peck on the cheek. "Making all kinds of noise, for that matter. Dinner's almost ready. You've been catnapping, Robert. Hands any better tonight?"

He glanced indifferently at his gnarled and swollen fingers. "They're all right. How did you meeting go?"

"Fine." She took a breath on the short fib, and then managed to smile cheerfully at him. "Now, did you have John over for a game of cribbage this afternoon? Did Mrs. Grenalda get to the windows?"

As she spoke, Leigh continued preparing dinner. Wearing a lime-green cotton sundress, she added a splash of color to the dark red brick and chrome kitchen. At home with Robert, who was the closet thing to family she had, she cast off her CPA "disguise." Her hair was loose about her shoulders, swirling in rich, sensual color with every movement. Barefoot and bare-legged, she moved with supple grace around the kitchen. But now, after the interview with Brian Hathaway, there was perhaps a forced brightness in her amber-flecked eyes as she tried to hide her distress from the perceptive Robert.

"Mrs. Grenalda says you'll have to get someone else to do the windows," Robert replied. "She says you never hired her to do the heavy work. I told her that if I was eighty-two and full of arthritis and could wash a few windows, she certainly—"

"You wash any windows in this house and you'll find out what trouble is," Leigh scolded. "If I ever catch you . . ."

"I can't just sit all day."

"I've never seen you sit all day. You wouldn't know how to if you tried," she retorted "But that doesn't mean you have to take on heavy projects like windows."

"Don't start. It's a clear case of the pot calling the kettle black," he said acerbically.

"You're getting sassier every year," Leigh complained ruefully, and he chuckled.

Leigh thought fondly that she could not imagine her life without Robert. He'd been around since before she was born, a butler then, and uniformed in stiff black, which reflected the aura of status, wealth, and influence that her mother had valued so highly. Robert had no family, but Leigh's father had provided him with both a pension and the promise of a home for life. He lived in a two-room apartment off the kitchen, which suited his independent nature very well.

Leigh's father had died when she was ten, and her mother and stepfather had been killed in an accident when she was just nineteen. Without any other close relatives, Leigh considered Robert as a sort of adopted grandfather, a role he assumed with gusto—scolding, disapproving, fussing over her until she came very close to exasperation. But then he would turn around and complain that she treated him exactly the same way.

"You've got a doctor's appointment at two tomorrow," Leigh reminded him suddenly. "I'll have lunch at work, but

I'll be home to pick you up by one-thirty."

His deeply lined face wrinkled still further. "You made the appointment, you keep it," he grumbled.

"Robert," she started to scold.

"I already know there's nothing to be done, Leigh. Hearts don't last forever, you know, and you needn't look so stricken. I haven't any intention of dying until I see you settled."

"Then I shall never settle," Leigh answered lightly, but her heart felt leaden whenever she thought of something happening to Robert. The doctor had already said that his heart was weak, but that there was no such thing as valid forecasting for a man of Robert's age. The doctor had told her this, he said, because she struck him as the sort of woman who could face facts.

And she was. Her training and education had been her chief legacy from her mother. Andrea Sexton had wanted to raise a daughter who was perfect by her own standards— clever, capable, independent, and invulnerable. She had never dried a tear, nor allowed an ounce of sentimentality in Leigh.

Leigh had been grateful for that upbringing. When she was just seventeen she'd thought her world was over, had even wanted it to be, but that independence had given her strength. At twenty-five, she was managing the not inconsiderable fortune she had inherited; had already directed her own education through the licensing as a CPA, and had been living a very private, secluded, but happy life . . . until the longing for a child had grown into more than a nighttime dream, had become an obsession that haunted her waking hours as well. It had intensified after the doctor had warned her of Robert's precarious hold on life. The thought of living alone in this large house year after year, with no one to care for and no one to care for her, seemed a bleak, sterile existence to Leigh.

"I thought you were invited out tonight," Robert interrupted her thoughts.

She rose from the dinner table. "Want some ice cream?" she asked as she set the dishes on the counter.

"I thought that gal Marjorie from work asked you to a party tonight," Robert repeated obstinately.

Leigh shook her head at him. "I've been so busy I haven't had a chance to do my own accounting lately."

"Then come home early," he suggested dryly. "What are you going to wear?"

"Pajamas and a robe," she retorted.

"Fine," he said amiably. "I'm sure you'll be a hit."

She chuckled with him. "Why," she complained, "are you always trying to get rid of me? What's wrong with spending an evening at home? I'm out all the time."

"You're at work all the time. Or shopping, or going to a class. But when an invitation to a party comes along," he continued, "suddenly you're too tired. You don't look tired. It's not that long since you were a teenager, you know, with all those boys hanging around. I know. My windows were off the kitchen. I used to count the minutes from the time your date parked the car in the driveway until you came in."

Leigh leaned forward, cupping her chin in the palms of her hands. "You didn't *spy!*" she said wickedly.

"I did."

"Pretty wild at sixteen, was I? It seems to me that was the year I discovered for absolute certain that babies don't come out of belly buttons. Not that I discovered that in the backseat of a car."

Robert's teasing expression faded slowly, and just as slowly he shook his head at her. "Damn it, Leigh, who do you think you're fooling?" he asked sadly. "I may not know the whole story, but it's time you were over it. I think you know that, too."

Instantly, there was a lump in her throat, a terrible sense of guilt. A man of eighty-two with a weak heart didn't need any additional worries, and she knew Robert was worried about her. She had tried to forget the past; four years ago, as a senior at college, she had even thought herself in love and had tried—and failed miserably—to purge the nightmare of David Hines once and for all. She couldn't go through that again, couldn't date and go to parties where she would meet eligible men, not even to please Robert. "You just want to be godfather to a whole host of children," she accused him lightly, desperately trying to get the smile on his face again. "The only thing really holding me back is the thought of twins. Dad was a twin, you know, and I think his granddad—"

"Yes. It's easy to get you on the subject of children. I had in mind that you should forget nurseries for a bit and concentrate on first things first—like the man," Robert replied dryly.

"I'd marry you, sweetheart, if you'd ask me." She blinked her eyelashes at him provocatively.

"Go on with you!" he chortled, but Leigh could see he was diverted. She reached over and hugged him with all the warmth of an affectionate nature that had no other outlet: just Robert, and the dream of a child. Love swelled in her so overwhelmingly that she felt tears in her eyes. In spite of Andrea's training, Leigh was more her father's daughter than her mother's. She needed to love, craved the freedom to give from her soul. She wanted a child, almost more than her life.

She had tried once to love a man, but never again. She had so hoped that Peter would be the answer to her prayers for a cure. Peter—blond, serious, gentle Peter. He'd started pursuing her when they were both sophomores at the University of Chicago, and two years later she'd finally agreed to have a dinner with him. She'd had a wonderful time that night, the first of many. He was husband material, father material, so gentle and affectionate; and yet he never pushed her sexually.

She knew he loved her and wanted to make love with her. He was so good to her, and she felt such contentment just being with him—real affection, shared interests. After a time, she knew it wasn't fair to keep insisting on a purely platonic relationship. He'd rarely stirred any real fears, partly because he never pushed her and partly because she felt no passion for him. Passion wasn't what she wanted in a relationship, and Peter in so many ways *was*.

Yet the night she agreed to sleep with him turned into another nightmare. Perhaps it was partly his inexperience, partly her own lack of sexual attraction toward him. Or maybe it was true what he had said afterward: that she was frigid. All she knew was that she found his wet kisses and clumsy groping all too reminiscent of the night her stepfather, David Hines, had tried to violate her. And yet she endured it all in rigid silence, reminding herself that this was not David but Peter—good, dear Peter who loved her and whom she thought she loved enough to go to bed with. She had tried to distract herself from what he was doing, but at his entry into her unwilling body, she had screamed out in pain and dug her nails into his back. Peter had thought it was the frenzy of passion, until afterward when she lay on the bed in his apartment sobbing and pleading with him not to touch her again, just to leave her alone.

She had seen the hurt in his eyes, and then the hardness as he ground out the words, "You might have told me you were frigid!"

She hadn't been able to explain. Wanting only to escape from him, she had quickly dressed and fled back to the security of the home she shared with Robert. Fortunately, Robert had been asleep and hadn't seen her disheveled state or her tears. By morning, she had been composed again, and a few weeks later, when he asked about that "nice fellow you were seeing," she was able to convince him of her indifference, dismissing the break-up as "just one of those things."

She closed her eyes, refusing to remember anymore. She'd hurt Peter, and badly, that was all. A man who'd meant her no harm, a good friend forever lost. Never again, Leigh had told herself. Yet the need to love was there, an ever-present ache. And so she had conceived the dream of a child.

August passed into September, bringing a measure of coolness. Autumn had always been Leigh's favorite season; she loved the fresh crisp days, the color of the leaves just beginning to change, the early evenings that invited a fire in the hearth. She welcomed the brisk spurts of energy that lay dormant in the lazy summer months, and announced to Robert that the second week in September was perfect for fall cleaning. Robert grumbled that Leigh was washing the paint off the walls, that he couldn't find anything in the cupboards, that he couldn't walk into a room without stumbling because the furniture was rearranged everywhere.

"Why can't you hire someone to do all this? It's too much for you after working all day," he argued. Which it was, but Robert had no way of understanding that rigorous physical work was the only thing that could take her mind off the baby that was never to be. There had been no phone call from Brian Hathaway; she had given up hope of ever receiving one. Only total exhaustion could sweep the disappointment from her mind.

But by Wednesday, she had accomplished better than a week's worth of cleaning, from the ceilings to the silver. If Robert was mentally weary of household upsets, Leigh had been driving herself to the point of collapse. They had eaten a light dinner after she had tackled the draperies, and that was after she'd worked a nine-hour day at White's. By the time Robert had retired to his apartment, she could barely limp upstairs for a very long soak in a scented tub. Afterward, she donned a simple white robe and padded downstairs in her bare feet, intent on doing nothing more than relaxing on the couch in the library with a good book.

It was a perfect occupation for someone who could barely move a muscle, but by the time she'd wedged some pillows behind her head and curled into a completely comfortable position, a little catnap seemed an even better idea. She had a fire going in the grate, and the only other light in the room was her reading lamp; the night was so quiet and the flickering shadows so mesmerizing...

The doorbell shattered the stillness some fifteen minutes later. Leigh's eyes fluttered open willingly enough, but the bell rang a second time before she could rouse herself from a feeling of sleepy disorientation. She'd just put one bare foot on the carpet when she heard Robert's, "It's all right, Leigh; I've got it. I was in the kitchen anyway. Though who the devil..."

"I'm in the library, Robert." She yawned, stretching lazily, shaking herself out of that somnolent, lazy feeling. She was expecting no one, but it wasn't unusual for Robert to invite a crony over for an evening of cribbage—and then forget having extended the invitation. She reached for the book that had fallen to the floor and was thumbing through the pages to find her place when Robert appeared in the doorway.

"Leigh," he said brightly, "the caller is for you. A Mr. Hathaway. He says you know him."

Her hands stilled on the novel in her lap. Robert was gloating like a two-year-old who'd been given a giant lollipop. Behind him, in the shadows, a pair of glittering black eyes stared intently at her through the softly lit room. Wearing a dark charcoal suit, with his bronzed complexion and dark hair, Brian Hathaway again reminded her of an Indian, proud and erect and silent, no expression visible on the broad planes of his face.

For a moment she couldn't seem to move. Her heart was racing out of control; he brought it with him, the primitive, sheerly sexual apprehension she'd been unable to control in his presence before. But almost immediately another emotion overwhelmed her, a sheer burst of joy. The child could be the only reason he was here. With a little indrawn breath, Leigh put her bare feet on the floor and stood up, hurriedly brushing back her sleep-tousled hair as she did so. Barefoot, she approached him with a poise that insisted she was just as impeccably dressed as he was. Deliberately, she forced her hand ahead of her. "Mr. Hathaway," she said formally.

He took her hand, enclosing her small palm in his larger one and keeping it. "You don't look anything like your sister, Red." Lazily, he took in all of her, from the bare toes to the barely concealed curves of her figure to the sensuous tumble of hair. With the fire as a backdrop, her hair took on golden highlights, the flame of a naturally warm and vibrantly alluring woman. And once his eyes took in that image, they held it, never leaving her face.

Robert coughed in the background. "Leigh doesn't have a sister, Mr. Hathaway," he said hesitantly.

"He's teasing, Robert," Leigh said evenly. "The last time he saw me I looked a little different."

"Of course, I did get a glimpse of you without your glasses," he reminded her lightly, "but this time I'm glimpsing . . . much more."

Her hand was released, too slowly, and she reacted immediately by folding closed the lapels of her robe. She forced a smile, willing herself not to look away from him. She was not going to fumble it, not this time. "Robert, would you entertain Mr. Hathaway for a moment while I put something on?"

"Of course, of course." Robert was grinning from ear to

ear. Leigh could well imagine the inquisition Brian was about to be put through. She had a moment's hesitation about leaving them together, but quickly decided even that was preferable to standing there any longer in her present state of undress.

Once out of sight, she vaulted the stairs two at a time, opening her dresser drawers in a flurry of action. Less than ten minutes later she descended the stairs in a black cowl-necked sweater and white wool pants, her hair brushed smoothly back from her forehead and flowing loosely behind her. Conservative colors always made her feel more comfortable, yet in her haste she was not sure she had chosen well. The black cashmere skimmed the firm mold of her breasts, the white slacks followed the slim curve of her hips a little too faithfully; and then, stark colors rather inevitably drew attention to her flaming halo of hair. Still, she forgot all about clothes when she found the library empty. Nothing mattered if he'd left, if he wasn't to give her the child she craved after all. She started breathing again when she saw the lights in the living room.

The room was decorated in pastel blues and gold, a woman's room entirely. It had been a long time since any man had been in there. Robert favored his own apartment in the evenings, and Peter had only been in it once or twice while waiting for her to come downstairs. Brian looked very much out of place amid Andrea Sexton's collection of bric-a-brac and fragile antiques. He was standing, hands in pockets, staring out the darkened window, and Robert was no-where in sight. The traitor, Leigh decided ruefully, had probably had a dreadful time deciding whether to stay and grill the tall dark stranger or to disappear so Leigh could be alone with him.

"Mr. Hathaway?" He turned to face her. "Since you're here, you must have decided to—"

"I'm thirsty as the devil," he interrupted lazily. When he smiled, he had a strangely compelling charisma. It was easy to see how he had gotten his reputation for leading ladies anywhere but to the altar.

But Leigh was not susceptible. "You *must* be here about the child."

"And if I say no, does that mean I no longer rate a drink?"

She sighed. "If I give you a drink will you say yes?" she demanded.

"Oh, I'm here to say yes, Leigh," he declared, "but with a slight change of terms."

Chapter 3

HER SMILE WAS radiant, and the appreciation in Brian's eyes told her that she was transformed into the radiant beauty Robert always told her she was. *"Any* terms, Mr. Hathaway." Swiftly the smile faded. "Unless you mean . . .?"

"I came to discuss making babies, Red, yes. But not sleeping with you."

Relieved, she crossed the room rapidly to the white French Provincial bar. "I don't know what you drink, but if I could serve you liquid gold . . . I never, *never* really believed you'd call!" She knew her giddy elation was showing, and she just couldn't seem to care. "Scotch? Whiskey? Cognac? Wine?" She glanced back up at him after rattling off the selection from behind the bar. "Is something wrong?"

His palm was worrying the nape of his neck as he stared at her, just the trace of an enigmatic smile on his lips. "I don't know what happened to the sexless CPA, Red, but it's going to take a little getting used to."

"Pardon?"

"You're a beautiful woman, Leigh. And you wear quite a different expression when you're working."

She stiffened.

"Scotch, straight," he requested. "And you'd better get one for yourself. You have yet to hear my terms."

But that didn't matter, as long as he didn't expect her to sleep with him—and he'd already clarified that point. She poured his scotch, keeping her eyes lowered, and just as quickly poured a glass of Beaujolais for herself before quietly edging out from behind the bar. Her exuberance faded a little. He hadn't taken his eyes off her since she'd entered, and she was glad for the wine.

"Sit down," she suggested softly.

He chose the center of the couch, his arms easily spanning the length of it, his foot crossed over one knee. He was perfectly relaxed, she thought fleetingly, while her heart was still thumping erratically. She felt joy. And disquiet. An uncomfortable blend. Taking her drink with her, she sat across from him in a pale blue brocade chair and waited. He didn't waste any time.

"First, Leigh, I'll tell you why your contract was nonsense, from both our points of view. From mine: at any time you could reveal my name, and all I could do would be to sue you for breach of contract; but obviously, the damage would already have been done. For yourself: you wanted the contract to insure that the prospective father wouldn't involve himself in the child's life. Sorry, Red, but it can't be done. As a point of honor, maybe, but these days the courts are very sympathetic to fathers who want to be involved with their kids. Besides, isn't a child entitled to the love of *both* parents? Were you planning to pose as a widow or divorcée—and didn't you realize that at some point the child would see through the ruse? And further, you haven't the right to deny your child a source of caretaking, if something happened to you." He paused. "But although your original idea was half-baked, I had reasons of my own for being interested in it—with modifications, which I'm here to discuss with you."

He leaned forward and sipped his scotch, staring at her over the amber liquid. "I come from a family that all but worships children, Red, even if domesticity isn't the personal lifestyle I've chosen, so I took your problem seriously. When I thought about it . . . you're obviously young and single and clearly want to stay that way." He hesitated. "It's not that I don't appreciate different lifestyles, but if I were going to be involved, I had to have some assurance that the child would at least have a basically healthy environment, some assurance that you could provide—"

"But I told you I have money."

"Not good enough," he said curtly. At his direct gaze, she looked away, staring broodingly out the living-room window. "You came across as a cold and emotionless woman, Red. All business. I liked that in you as far as your work went, but when I thought of an emotional environment for my child . . ."

She nodded, almost shocked to find herself on the same wavelength with him. "I never meant to give you that impression—that I had no emotional warmth to give a child. I . . ." She hesitated. "I thought—"

"You wanted to be very sure I understood you weren't asking for an affair," he finished for her curtly. "Especially after the, er, misunderstanding that occurred."

Just the faintest flush coraled her cheeks. She was not the woman he thought she was; she could see it in that look of his. He set his glass down, continuing, "So I found out a few things about you. Your father was Gerald Sexton, a man who had a genius for buying the right piece of land at the right time. Thanks to him, you've got a trust set up that should last you a lifetime. But you've never been content with that kind of security. You've worked like hell to enhance your financial position, and I can almost see why. If it had been up to your stepfather, David Hines, he'd have spent every penny of that not inconsiderable trust. But he and your mother died in a car accident when you turned nineteen."

Her hands gripped the glass, a curtain of red-gold hair blocking her eyes from him. He *couldn't* have found out . . .

"As for you, personally—you knew your multiplication tables at four. You were one smart and sassy child, with every ounce of spirit and independence encouraged. No rules—but not spoiled, not showered with expensive gifts and toys. In high school you were crowned prom queen more than once, and partied with the young set at the country club, so clearly you weren't always averse to the male of the species, Red," he added with a twist of dry humor. "By the time I uncovered that much, I was hours past worrying about your emotional stability. In fact, the opposite was true. I was becoming intrigued with the total picture."

She brushed her hair back from her forehead and faced him again, keeping her face a cameo mold of stillness. He leaned even farther forward, his forearms resting loosely on his thighs, his hands idly twisting the glass back and forth. "When your parents died, you changed your life completely. No more country-club amusements. You graduated *cum laude* from the University of Chicago, and were certified as a CPA in record time. The cold-blooded world of statistics seemed to suit you very well—and you're good at it, Red. People respect you. But no one seems to know a single personal detail about you; your private life is very private. I envy you that privacy," he added softly and tilted the glass to finish his drink.

"I don't understand," she said. There was a throbbing in her temples, a consistent dull ache. He had not found out anything about David Hines. He didn't realize that she had done all that late-night partying as a teenager because she was afraid to go home. Of course, there was no way he could have found out. Still, his attitude toward her tonight made her uneasy. His manner was deliberately relaxed, familiar, as if they were talking on the level of . . . friends. His low, husky voice in the silent room, the suggestive glimmer in his dark eyes, the taut sense of controlled sexuality in that special quietness of his . . . no, she thought bitterly, they could never be friends. She wished he would finish the preliminaries and get down to his modifications of her proposition so they could come to terms.

He stood up suddenly, and his eyes bored into hers as she forced herself to remain still. "There's no medical reason why you have to have the child by artificial insemination, is there?"

Panic gripped her. "I told you I wouldn't answer any personal questions, Mr. Hathaway. Surely—"

"I didn't think there was," he said flatly, just as if she

had answered his question. She stirred, suddenly as restless as he was. In the short silence that followed, he simply paced, finally stopping to lean back against a far wall, his face completely in shadow and his hands jammed into his pockets. "You've shut yourself off for a long time, Red, and there's only one likely explanation for that. The reason has to be a man. He was either a bastard or a saint, I've decided. A married lover you couldn't have? A fiance who died? So you want a child, but you don't want any other man—intimately. Isn't that your story?"

It was her turn to bolt from her chair, her face chalky. "How dare you—"

"I don't give a damn about your secerts, Leigh," he interrupted brusquely. "You can carry a torch for whomever you like. That's your business."

Confused, she stared up into the shadows at him. He seemed so tall and forbiddingly powerful, able to see her clearly in the circle of lamplight while she could barely make out his features.

"You're independent to a fault, Red," he said very, very slowly. "A fault we share. Conventions mean nothing to you—something else we share. You want no permanent commitment to a member of the opposite sex—and neither do I. You've also got a good brain and a very alluring softspoken way about you. Your determination to have a baby this way is nutty as hell, but I admire your courage. You're completely different from any woman I've ever known, and I know a lot of women—too many of whom are trying to lead me to the altar." He paused. "Why don't you get yourself another glass of wine," he said softly.

She shook her head wildly, and pivoted so that she was facing the window. She had a horrible feeling she knew what was coming.

His reflection was suddenly in the paned glass behind her. Like an Indian, he had moved without sound; like an Indian, he showed no expression. And as he approached, she felt his nearing sexuality like an internal drumbeat—a slow, insidious rhythm as menacing as it was powerful.

She whirled before he was close enough to touch her. He stopped, with a frown between his eyes, and rather than be subjected to his intense scrutiny she moved rapidly away to the bar and refilled her wineglass. "Mr. Hathaway," she began.

"Brian."

She shook her head.

"Leigh, that baby deserves a name."

She shook her head again and took a long draught of wine, setting her glass on the bar with trembling fingers. She felt caged; she hadn't felt so stifled in a long time. "You're not seriously suggesting..." She wouldn't pretend not to know what he was talking about. "No," she said simply.

Brian came to the opposite side of the bar and held out his glass for a refill. "Relax," he said quietly. "If there's anyone who should be skittish about the subject of marriage, Red, it's me. I'm thirty-five and have avoided that tie for more than a decade. I've never had the least urge to come home to curlers and ten o'clock headaches and boredom; in most marriages I've seen, the satin turns to cotton the day after the honeymoon."

"Your preference for a playboy's lifestyle is well known," she said caustically.

"I play the game fair, Red; I always have," he replied evenly. "I've never promised commitments I didn't intend to keep. But I'm tired of the scenes that keep occurring every time one of my lady friends gets it into her head that there's no reason why an unattached bachelor like me shouldn't marry her. A wife—a pregnant wife—a wife and child..."

"I see," she said coldly. "A wife and child would mean you *couldn't* marry someone else. But why don't you just marry one of your 'lady friends' as you call them?"

He shook his head. "I would have married a long time ago, if only for business reasons, if I thought I could find someone who shared my idiosyncratic concept of marriage. Respect, independence, determination, and honesty—with no demands made."

"No!" she said wildly.

"I wouldn't take anything away from your... past lover, Red. You don't have to sleep with me; I can get that else-where." His eyes bored into hers. "I'm talking about a marriage on terms we both understand. Not a fly-by-night arrangement, a legal marriage. I'm sick of eating in restaurants, coming home to a lonely apartment. A name for your child, protection—those things I can offer you. We'd have no emotional ties, just respect for each other, an objective ear on occasion. It's the one kind of marriage I believe I could live with, where two people might actually have a chance to fill one another's needs, without hurting or destroying each other."

"Brian . . ." But that last argument had pierced through the wall. He was talking about the only kind of marriage she could live with, too, and the word *protection* floated back to her—the child's name, the blunt promise that sex was easily available to him elsewhere, not important . . . And Robert would be so pleased—thrilled, in fact. She gave Brian a long look. She could not doubt that he meant every word he said; sincerity was in his eyes, his face, his posture.

She took a breath. He sounded so persuasive, but if ever a man personified virility, total domination, and control, it was Brian Hathaway. "You wouldn't consider—" she started softly.

"You can have your baby out of wedlock—but not by me, Red. It has to be marriage. I've tried to make it clear that I wouldn't infringe on whatever torch you're carrying. The kind of arrangement we're talking about would only work if we both really did feel the same way, if we both thought we stood to gain by it. Of course, a certain amount of keeping up appearances would be necessary. I've noticed how you get an attack of the vapors every time I touch you. It would certainly be impossible for both of us if you had hysterics every time our elbows happened to jostle over an occasional breakfast table."

"Don't be silly," Leigh said petulantly, furious with herself for having repeatedly revealed so much of herself to him.

With a sense of shock, she saw that he was buttoning his suit coat. He was done talking, then. He was free to walk out. There would be no baby, no longer even a hope of one, and all of it probably quickly forgotten by this dark stranger who seemed so perfect for her purposes.

"You may need a wife—a wife and child—for now,

Brian," she reflected aloud, "but later you might change your mind. Still," she considered, "if by then I were pregnant . . . the child means everything to me. It sounds crazy, but I could almost believe—"

"Nine months as a trial?" he broke in. "Your nine months, Leigh." Abruptly, he made for the door, saying she could have until Saturday to change her mind. He would pick her up at eleven, and they would iron out whatever else needed discussing. And then, he simply left, barely giving her the chance to say good night.

In a daze she took the two empty glasses to the kitchen and washed them out before wearily climbing the stairs to bed. She gathered the covers snugly around her, eager to put an end to a day that had been too long. Yet her eyes remained wide open in the darkness.

She seemed to be under the insane illusion that she was engaged to be married. And it *was* insane. Perhaps she had even wanted to be taken in by all that talk about honesty and respect; perhaps she had once considered those particular traits as critically important in a mate; perhaps she was even desperate to believe in trust, just to a degree . . . But could she really trust Brian Hathaway? From the first, he had thrown her off-balance as she had allowed no other man to do in years. His sexuality was so blatant, and the appraising perception of his eyes so disconcerting. It was impossible not to imagine how easily a man like that could overpower someone like her. She had a memory of another pair of arms that had forcibly held her, and they had not been nearly as strong as Brian's. A memory that filled her with fear and revulsion. But she wanted that baby. She needed to love; she needed to be needed. Was that so very wrong? She had feared that her need was a selfish one, but after much soul-searching she'd concluded that she had a great deal of love and cherishing and warmth to give, and enough character within herself to encourage spirit, nor dependence, in a child.

She closed her eyes, desperately trying to think. She'd never liked domineering men, and Brian Hathaway certainly was that. He was also arrogant, uncannily perceptive, egotistical . . . and yet, he had been honest. She believed that. The man's integrity—his own brand—was not to be doubted.

It was all so easy, really. He was nothing like Peter; it was inconceivable that she could hurt him. And he was offering all and more than she wanted. The only real question was whether she would be able to trust him not to touch her. But Robert would be there; they would not have to see each other very often; and perhaps in time that trust... *No!*

Yet the image of the child persuaded her, lulling her fears, just before sleep finally came.

Chapter 4

SATURDAY MORNING WAS misty and cool. A few minutes before eleven, Leigh walked out onto the back patio, wanting a last breath of fresh air to steady her nerves. Her hair, a mixture of chestnut and fire in the sunlight, whispered against her cheeks in the breeze. She was dressed for her meeting with Brian as she rarely dressed: a pale saffron jersey dress with a looped gold belt that cinched her waist. The color set off her eyes, just as the fit of the dress enhanced the sensuous curves of her figure. The makeup she wore had been carefully applied; a touch of eyeshadow and mascara to deepen the amber tint of her eyes; blusher to accent the line of cheekbone; lipstick to emphasize the exact curve of her mouth. "A lovely woman," Robert had approvingly labeled her.

For a moment, she closed her eyes, hearing the crackle of newly turned leaves in the wind. She had made no clear-cut decision in the four days since she'd seen Brian. She had told herself to wait and see him again. To see . . . what

31

she could handle. And dressing attractively was one way to test that.

When she opened her eyes and turned around, he was there. There had been no sound of footsteps, or of his car. In brown cords and a loose brown-and-gold velour shirt, he looked like a very different man . . . yet not necessarily an easier one to deal with. The casual clothes, if anything, only accentuated the disturbingly masculine aura of control that surrounded him.

"Good morning." His black eyes took in her face and dress before moving on to the landscape around him. He passed, just that quickly, his first test.

The cement patio ended in steps leading down a slanting terraced lawn, with an orchard of mixed fruit trees on the distant left, a vegetable and flower garden on the right. The grounds had never been formally landscaped, but Leigh had spent a great deal of time and effort on the garden and lawn, and the effect always pleased her.

"About three acres?" he questioned.

She nodded. "Back here. With the woods as you come into the drive, it's just under five." Her tone was polite, distant. She could feel her emotions rising to the surface, an automatic response to his mere presence—defensiveness, antagonism, apprehension—and willed herself to remain calm.

"Have you changed your mind, Leigh?" he asked bluntly.

She looked away from him. "I still don't know about the marriage," she admitted honestly. "But there's no question about my wanting a child."

"There won't be one without the other—not if you want me involved." There was just the hint of a rebuke, and she flushed.

"I understand that," she said coolly.

"Would you like some coffee?" Robert's beaming face appeared at the French doors, taking in the pair of them standing together. "I just made a fresh pot for myself."

"No thanks, Robert. We're off," Brian answered easily. He moved briskly then, forcing Leigh ahead of him into the library, and headed for the front door. Robert followed, hovering, as if by looking at them he could discover a clue to the exact nature of their relationship, which Leigh had refused to define for him over the last few days. It seemed that Brian understood. "I'll have your girl back before dinner, Robert, if that suits?"

It seemed just the line Robert had been waiting for. "I wouldn't take it kindly if anything should happen to her." He had to look up almost a full foot into Brian's face to say it, and involuntarily Leigh smiled. For a protector, Robert lacked both height and youth, but if Brian made fun of him . . .

"I promise you she'll be safe with me," he said gravely.

"That's fine then." Robert was satisfied. "Have a good time, sweetheart. God knows it'll be peaceful without you," he added acerbically. She knew he was referring to her noisy cleaning onslaught, and she smiled again. With a gallant flourish, Brian opened the door for her and she stepped out. Brian had unknowingly passed another test, accepting Robert without mockery or even comment.

The next ten minutes passed in silence, and by then Leigh and Brian were on one of Chicago's busiest freeways. "What kind of car is this?" she finally asked.

"A Morgan."

"I've never heard an engine with quite that kind of sound before." That was true; it still seemed strange that she hadn't even heard his approach to the house.

"Am I to take it that you know something about engines?" Brian asked skeptically. "Or is this a round of polite conversation?"

His rudeness struck her as more honest than abrasive, and she relaxed perceptibly. She really didn't want to make small talk either.

It was another twenty minutes before he pulled into a parking lot next to one of Chicago's more expensive highrises. They were almost directly in the center of town, close to Brian's work and close to the art galleries and museums and department stores that Leigh was familiar with. She opened her own door, and without comment followed him into the building and elevator, up to the fifteenth floor. He fitted the key into the lock and motioned her inside.

"Look around," he suggested. "Among other things, we'll have to talk about where we want to live. I think you'll find that my apartment has ample room."

The subject had fleetingly occurred to her. Then as now, next to everything else, it had seemed unimportant. Simple curiosity overruled her instinctive disquiet at being alone with Brian in his apartment, and obediently she wandered around exploring. To the left of the entrance was a sunny yellow kitchen, smaller than Leigh's but more efficiently arranged. There was also a dining room, and to the right of it four small bedrooms. Robert could have his own suite; and there would still be a bedroom for her and one for the baby. And then there was Brian's study and the master bedroom: she only opened the doors and closed them quickly once they'd been identified for what they were. From there, she paused at the living-room threshold.

With background colors of black and white, the living room was spacious and starkly contemporary. The floor was highly polished wood, with an unbelievably soft and furry black-and-white rug large enough to accommodate two couches and a glass coffee table. A stereo unit took up most of one wall, and a double set of glass doors led onto a small balcony. There wasn't a hint of anything feminine about the room, but it was both tastefully and attractively done.

"Well?" Brian asked finally. "Shall we fight out where we're going to live?"

She gave him a ghost of a smile. "Of course not," she said mildly. "We can live here if you want to. It doesn't make any difference to me, as long as there's room enough for Robert and the baby. In the long run, I wouldn't choose to raise a child in the middle of a city, but we needn't worry about that for the moment."

He frowned, as if her answer had been both unexpected and somehow unwelcome. She could make nothing of that, nor of his taciturn moodiness this morning. If he had changed his mind, he need only say so. From her viewpoint, she had immediately realized that any arrangement they made would require elements of compromise and flexibility; as she had more to gain, she was certainly willing to give more as well.

"Do you want coffee, Leigh, or some lunch?"

She wanted both, and they moved into the kitchen. Brian made salami sandwiches, while Leigh continued to poke around cupboards, learning the layout of the room. When they were seated at the kitchen table, he said, "I rather thought you'd want to stay in your own house."

She could hardly explain that, much as she loved her home, there were also unpleasant memories that she could never escape as long as she lived there. Instead, she spoke of practical matters: the costs of heating and maintaining an older home; her dislike of having to hire help to run the house when she would prefer being able to cope on her own. And Robert didn't care where he lived; for that matter, it would be easier for him in the city, where he had friends of long standing whose age made it difficult for them to travel back and forth to her house in the suburbs. "Anyway, we're hardly talking about a permanent commitment to a specific home, are we? I mean, we don't even know if marriage with us would work a month, much less a lifetime," she said frankly. "I have to admit I'm a little disappointed, though."

"Disappointed? Why?"

"I was hoping you lived in one of your own houses. One that you designed."

"Just what do you know of my houses?" he asked curiously.

She hesitated, then took a small sip of coffee. "Did you forget I had access to all your books the four weeks I worked for your firm? Although I have to admit, if anyone had questioned why I was in the sepia room . . ."

His eyebrows raised. "Why on earth were you?"

She gave him a lazy grin. "To find out what kind of man you were. You build honest buildings, Brian. I would never have approached you otherwise."

He choked a little on his sandwich. "Honest buildings," he repeated dryly. "What the devil does that mean?"

She shook her head. "If you're not careful, we'll find ourselves making polite conversation, Brian." It was a tentative try at being comfortable around him, a hint of teasing. She was rewarded with a smile so disarming that she felt her heart skip a beat. And then he was all business again.

"I'm afraid we're going to have to disagree—on the subject of where we live, that is. I would prefer to live in your house. Frankly, you surprised me. I thought you would automatically want to stay at your place."

"Then why did you even bring me here?" she asked curiously.

"To let you win the first round of arguments," he said bluntly. "I thought you would insist on your own home, and I would give in. But then I would have an advantage on the next issue."

"Oh. Well . . ." She finished her sandwich, and then concentrated on her coffee.

"Your house is bigger, and we would be less likely to get in each other's way," he continued. "You're already settled there, and so is Robert. The cost of running the place hardly matters. You've got both a study and a library downstairs, so it won't matter if I take one of them over. And I like the land around the place; I'm sick of concrete."

"All right, we'll live there," Leigh said affably. "Why don't you just keep this place, too, so that you have a place for your little . . ."

His eyes met hers, instant black lightning. "As long as we're not talking about *your* private life, you can be blunt enough, can't you, Red?" he said shortly.

She didn't answer. She wished she had his ability to maintain a totally impassive face for hours at a time. She had no way of judging his emotions at all, beyond what he said and what he communicated with his eyes, and both his words and his gaze seemed to have a disconcerting effect on her senses.

As if to reinforce that effect, he changed the subject. "I've got the marriage license. As soon as we get the ceremony over with, we can get on with the child."

Was that where he wanted the advantage? "No," she said firmly. "First I want to be sure I *can* get pregnant. Otherwise, there would be no reason at all for me to get married."

"But if you conceive first, it won't be a full-term baby."

"A month 'premature' wouldn't matter."

There was a moment's silence, and then Brian gave a short, harsh chuckle. "I'm still having difficulty seeing myself as an advocate for marriage." He got up and poured himself a second cup of coffee, turning cold eyes in her direction. "To look at you, Red, you're as soft and vulnerable as a kitten. But I'm not sure I'd want to face you across a boardroom when you get that look in your eyes."

"I—"

"If you want *my* child," he interrupted sharply, "it will be a full-term, nine-month baby. The ceremony can be secret, but it must precede the pregnancy. As a concession to you, we won't announce the marriage until you're pregnant. If we make no baby, we'll set new terms. The ceremony takes less than ten minutes when there's no rigmarole, and to my knowledge, you sweet little coward, it doesn't hurt a bit."

She flushed at his sarcasm, and his "sweet" had a wasp-like sting to it. "You can't mean you would actually withdraw your offer if—"

"I would."

With characteristic arrogance, he was insisting that she commit on his terms or forget the whole thing. To live her life in a stark, lonely vacuum, or to take the chance offered to have a child and make a real home . . . with a vibrantly sensual, totally enigmatic man, who for some strange reason actually believed they'd suit each other. But, would she ever have another chance? "You promise, of course," Leigh said gravely, "that the ceremony doesn't hurt?"

His smile transformed his impassive features and gentled the sharpness in his eyes. "You give in gracefully, lady. I'm glad," he added quietly.

Leigh twisted her fingers together beneath the table, disarmed by the compliment. "So, what's the next step?" she asked briskly.

"I'll take care of the wedding; you take care of the doctor. The next question is timing."

"All right." But that suddenly wasn't going to be any easier a subject. "If you have any questions about the doctor, Brian, I researched the fertility field quite thoroughly. Dr. Janet Hensley—"

"Knowing you, Red, and your feelings on this subject, I'm sure you meticulously researched her medical and ethical credentials."

"Yes. Well . . ." Her eyes, which had been thoughtfully staring into the last dregs of her coffee cup, suddenly raised to meet his. "Her ethics are the point, Brian. You can't just walk in to a really good doctor, prove to be . . . healthy, and still request . . ." She saw his eyes suddenly narrow, but she didn't stop talking. Lying went against her instincts: It hadn't been easy with the doctor; and with Brian, she refused to lie, regardless of his reaction. Quietly, she admitted that she had led Dr. Hensley to believe she was married, that her husband was . . . incapable, though they both wanted a child, that they had agreed on a donor . . .

"I don't like made-up stories, Leigh," Brian interrupted grimly.

She felt strangely hungry for his teasing "Red," instead of the abrasive way he spoke her given name. "I didn't believe she would take me on any other way," she admitted in a low voice. "I did what I had to do, Brian. I would have done almost anything."

The phrase echoed in that short silence. For no reason she could fathom, his look suddenly softened on hers. "All right, Red," he said finally, and she knew that the subject was buried. She took a breath.

"As for timing, it's the first or second of October or else we have to wait another month. Next week, in other words. All you have to do is go to the office the same day and—"

"You mean you go into one room and I go into another," he cut in sardonically. "And when we both come out . . ." A burst of laughter, husky and masculine, was accompanied by a shake of his head. "Really, Red, it would be a lot easier to handle the normal way."

It was there suddenly, the panic she'd felt when she first met him, like a splintering of glass inside. She stood up, preparing to leave.

"Oh, for heaven's sake! Listen here," he said sharply. "Listen and sit down!" She did, at the very edge of the chair. "The fact is," he said disgustedly, "I can't think of anything much more degrading than this situation you've outlined— a man in one room and a woman in another, and strangers running back and forth with test tubes. The lack of privacy, if nothing else . . ."

He sighed at her expression. "Red, I don't want to sleep with you," he said harshly. "I want peace and freedom out of this marriage, not clinging ties. But the whole experience would be quicker, more private, and a great deal less distasteful than that scene in the doctor's office—which, after all, may have to be repeated more than one time. I—"

"Don't," she said tightly. "Don't say any more." She struggled inwardly to gain control. The images were all so easily there, brought on by his suggestion of sex for *her* sake: images of naked flesh and pain and the sound of crying.

She managed to look back at him, finally. "If you want to call it off, I can certainly understand. We're just so...different." She hesitated. "For that matter, I have a little fuel to add to the fire."

"What?"

"It's Robert. He hasn't long to live, and, well, he's all I have. He's got his heart set on seeing me settled. He isn't around much, really; he disappears to his room most nights by seven. But I would have to ask you not to disillusion him—not to lie, but if you do cross paths, to simply be careful about what you say."

"You don't think the illusion of newlyweds might be difficult to maintain with separate bedrooms?" Brian inquired dryly.

"He hasn't been upstairs in years because of his arthritis. There would be no reason for him to know that."

"Well, my mother and Robert sound like two of a kind. She's not a person one can explain this sort of marriage to. You wouldn't have to cross paths often, either—my family lives in Minnesota—but if and when you do, she'll be delighted at the idea of you and the marriage and the grandchild. Home, children...you're just the image of the perfect wife."

His tone was so heavily sarcastic that it almost made Leigh flinch.

"Come here, Red."

Her eyes widened at the unmistakable command, couched in misleading gentleness.

"Why?" she asked warily. She stood up again, but made no move to approach him.

"Because I keep getting the ridiculous idea that you're afraid of me. If we're going to be around other people occasionally, I think we'd better establish the rules of the game." In a few long strides, he had reached her side, grabbed her arm, and propelled her toward the door. "Damn it, if you don't quit looking at me like that . . . I like my women warm and willing, Red, get that through your head. We're going for a walk. There are two million people walking around Chicago. Do you think you could manage to feel safe enough with me out there?"

But they did not go for a walk. Brian drove the short distance to the Field Museum instead, and with busloads of senior citizens, uniformed schoolchildren, families, and groups of teenagers, they stood in line to pay the entrance fee. It had become a sultry September afternoon, perfect for an outing, and the museum was swarming with people.

When they were finally through the entrance doors, Brian scanned the massive lobby and its clusters of people with an expression of satisfaction. Loosely resting his hands on his hips, he inquired gravely, "Dinosaurs or mummies?"

He was insane. "Mummies," she answered dryly.

He held out his hand, which she didn't take. "People do it all the time," he announced. "Fathers and daughters, brothers and sisters. I've even been known to take my secretary's arm on the rare occasion we have to cross a street together. There's nothing intimate about a hand. Five fingers—everyone has them."

She took his hand, more or less to shut him up. He was being insufferably patronizing, making her feel like an absolute fool for allowing him to glimpse emotions that no one had guessed at in years. And yes, of course there would be occasions in public when perhaps their hands would have to touch.

His palm was cool and dry, and once his fingers had closed over hers, consciousness of his touch, his male presence, sent a shivering pulse all through her, as if she were connected to an electric current. Not meeting his eyes, she simply walked with him, aware that he was nearly a full head taller than she was, that there was a faint but distinctly masculine scent about him, that he had the sort of magnetism that made other heads in the crowd—male and female— turn to look at them.

It had been a long time since she had stood that close to any man but Robert. She willed away the first moments of dread. Brian had gone out of his way to establish trust by setting the scene in a crowd. They wandered around, pausing at different exhibits, for the most part silently. Leigh felt a blend of amusement and simple relief at being ignored. It almost seemed that Brian had completely forgotten about her until, as she bent over a glass-tabled exhibit, her hair brushed in a wave over her eye. When she tried to untangle her hand from his to push it back, his hold on her tightened.

Unsmiling, Brian looked down at her, his own fingers brushing the strands from her face, tucking them behind her ear. "Do you have any idea how many people have stared at your hair, Red?" he questioned curiously. "That rich dark copper color . . ."

Confused and wary of his soft tone, she said shortly, "I wish you wouldn't call me Red!"

He shook his head at her. "Why the hell are you so skittish?" Deliberately, he wound an arm around her shoulder, drawing her close, reaching behind with his other hand to snatch hers. Her fingers curled in a fist; his own fingers covered her fist, preventing her from moving unless she wanted to make a graceless tussle in the crowd. "Can you believe it?" he whispered dryly. "Our shirts are touching. What's going to happen? You've never seen anyone do this before, of course."

She drew in a deep, furious breath. It was her own fault. If she hadn't been so foolish as to let him see that she was afraid of him, she doubted if he would have pressed for any physical contact at all. If she could only relax, prove to him . . .

It happened after a time. The stiff mannequin she had become relaxed somewhere between ancient lyres and Indian cultures, as her muscles protested against her rigid control. In reward, his viselike grip loosened, and his arm simply rested lightly on her shoulder, his fingers on occasion, perhaps by accident, brushing against her hair. The dread she had initially felt faded; the inner tension never quite disappeared, but to her surprise it was not altogether an unpleasant sensation. There was even a peculiarly enjoyable feeling of being encircled, protected; for a few moments she admitted to herself that she felt safer than she had in a long time. His arm was heavy; she was becoming slowly accustomed to his scent; and when he half-turned once, the weight of one of her breasts crushed against the hardness of his chest. He didn't seem to notice, and perhaps because of that Leigh did not instinctively jerk back. The warmth that flooded through her was more a result of sheer feminine awareness than panic.

By late afternoon they had checked out most of the exhibits, and most of the people seemed to be leaving the museum as dinnertime drew closer. Leigh felt pangs of hunger herself, but she was loath to say anything. She had no doubt that it would be back to their impersonal relationship once they left the museum, and that was what she wanted, of course. Still . . .

An unexpected confusion about her own feelings nagged inside as she allowed Brian to lead her into still another exhibition room. Although she'd often been to the museum as a child, she didn't remember the place: it was an exhibit of gems, and everywhere there was the sparkle and silence of brilliance—diamonds, rubies, emeralds, sapphires, opals, moonstones, tourmalines. She stopped before a particularly fantastic moonstone, huge and oval in shape, indescribable in its beauty, and glanced up to share an appreciative smile with Brian.

His black eyes were oddly warm, lazy. "I suppose you're going to want one of these stones for an engagement ring?" he questioned teasingly.

"No," she said quickly, her smile fading. "I really don't care much for jewelry, and I think under the circumstances the most we need to bother with would be simple gold bands."

He stiffened slightly, as if her answer hadn't pleased him, and shortly after that they headed down the stairway to end the afternoon's excursion. They were almost the last ones out of the museum, and it was nearing six-thirty when they reached the entrance doors.

Brian paused in the marble porch, and turned an unsuspecting Leigh to face him with both hands on her shoulders. "Shall we finish listing all the rules, Red?"

Like the brush of a feather, his lips came down on hers, soft and sure. It was over almost before it happened, leaving a familiar yet elusive taste on her lips. "A kiss for company," he explained sardonically. "It will seem pretty damn odd if we don't, on occasion."

Suddenly, his lips descended again, with only slightly more pressure. The taste, she discovered, was the lingering flavor of a mint he'd eaten earlier, and hinted at the taste of the man himself, a smooth, warm masculine flavor. But it was the feel of his hands on her shoulders that began the long, low shiver inside. Rules—his rules: the power of his hands . . . the way his black eyes stared intently down at her when his head bent back.

She knew the flicker of panic she felt must be reflected on her face, for a perplexed look came into his eyes. "A Christmasy sort of kiss," he explained, "for the holidays, when people are surrounding you and the presents are being handed out. That's an acceptable version, don't you think?"

No, she didn't think. Anything. A sudden, disquieting warmth was flooding her veins—as if she had just drunk a snifter of brandy.

"We'd better get all the rules out of the way, Red." The smile was deliberately teasing as he raised her limp arms and placed them around his neck, tucking his own behind her back. His next kiss forced her lips helplessly apart. Like a series of shocks, she felt the thick, heavy texture of his hair in her fingers, the graze of his thighs against her own, the touch of his splayed fingers at the small of her back. His mouth covered hers so completely that she had to breathe with him; she had to inhale that taste, that bittersweet flavor of possession. It was an assault on her senses of the gentlest kind, but an assault nonetheless. Fear and dread started to rise in her, but had no chance to surface before he pulled back, staring at her with a grave, puzzled expression. His eyes were like black fire, as if he'd found something he hadn't expected. That she was snow? Ice? "There are always those few souls left who believe in love, aren't there, Red?" he asked wryly. "My mother is a strong holdout for love and marriage; she'll need some convincing."

"Fine," she said faintly. Her knees felt wobbly, and it was going to take all the effort she could muster to just walk away without him knowing how she really felt. But at least it was done, and she hadn't fled. Yet the teasing light was completely gone from his eyes as he insistently reached for her again.

Altering her balance, he pressed her whole body deliberately to the length of him, far too expertly enclosing her before she could slip away. Her breasts were crushed against the soft velour of his shirt, and she could feel his heartbeat marking time with her own. His right hand traveled up her back, blazing a trail of sensual pressure as his left hand cradled her head. His mouth dipped down. He tasted her frantic little "no"; his tongue touched hers, very gently; and his fingers tangled in her hair, preventing her from breaking away. His lips lifted long enough to brush her eyes closed, and then came back to her mouth again, this time not gentle at all, but hard and hungry and starkly sexual in intent. His hips cradled hers. With a shock of sheer horror she realized he was not as immune to her sexually as she'd thought, that he was inviting her to...

The fear surfaced and exploded; her whole body suddenly trembled violently and she struggled to break away. He allowed their lips to separate, but kept his arms firmly around her for another moment. His voice was oddly ragged, almost hoarse. "Obviously, that was for Robert. A treat for him on occasion. You did say you want to be sure he thinks we're...happy, Leigh, didn't you?"

And then he let her go.

It wasn't for Robert. She didn't know what he was doing, but he wasn't merely listing rules. It was deliberate and cold-blooded and...With long strides, Brian had already hastened down the wide marble steps, and she had to run after him. Flushed and furious, she reached the car just ahead of him, managing to get inside and slam the door even before he could open it for her. He slid into the driver's seat meeting her eyes with an infuriatingly calm half-smile.

"I don't think there's much question that we set an exact standard of rules, do you, Red?" His barely suppressed chuckle grated like sandpaper, but then he glanced at his watch with a frown. "I think we both owe ourselves a dinner, but unfortunately, I already have an engagement and I'm late as it is."

"Good. If you're late, I would rather take a taxi home

anyway," Leigh said curtly, her hand on the car door handle.

He revved the engine, ignoring her. Before she could open the door, he had backed out of the parking space. For the next ten minutes, neither of them said a word. Traffic was thick, inevitably congested around Chicago's Loop. The gray haze of dusk marked the end of a long summer day. A chilly breeze was sweeping off Lake Michigan in marked contrast to the warmth of the earlier afternoon, and Leigh felt a chill sweep over her as well, inside and out. The tall, broad-shouldered figure at her side no longer seemed to offer her protection, but spelled danger instead. He was the Indian once again: remote, aloof, elementally alone. The antagonism she felt for him filled her, like a glass of bitter tea.

She almost jumped when he spoke.

"You know," he said casually, "something didn't quite jell there, Leigh. I've been under the impression that you either made a devil of a lot of wrong choices—and are as cynical as I am—or that you're carrying a torch, being faithful to a lover you can't forget. But back there...I would almost have thought you'd never been kissed before."

"Think again," Leigh said bitterly. "I've had enough experiences with men to last me a lifetime!"

He turned his eyes away from the road for a moment to study her averted face, and when his eyes returned to the traffic he was frowning, his fingers drumming an impatient tattoo against the steering wheel. Leigh sat as far away from him as possible for the rest of the half-hour drive home. Her face averted to the window, she stared at the houses and buildings and stores whirling by as if they were of intense interest to her. In fact, she barely saw them, and she could not help emitting an audible sigh of relief when she caught sight of the wrought-iron fence marking the boundaries of her property.

Before he'd even stopped the car, she had her right hand on the door handle, but he grasped her other wrist before she could escape. "You can hardly wait to get inside, can you, Red?" he demanded. "You're going for the four-minute mile to the closest pen and paper. Will the letter calling it off reach my office by Monday?"

Her lowered eyes spoke for themselves. His fingers

reached over and raised her chin. There was extra moisture in her eyes, not quite tears, blurring her vision. He was too close. "Listen," Brian said harshly. "I broke no faith with you, and I don't intend to. A few kisses hardly constitutes rape!"

"All right," she said softly, calmer now. She needed to believe him. Not for the sake of the child or the marriage; but for herself. She needed to trust someone.

"Do you want a promise? I would never force you to make love with me, Leigh. Is that black and white enough?"

"Yes," she admitted, and gave him a tremulous smile when he released her, her relief obvious. She hesitated. "Trust simply doesn't come easily. Perhaps in time."

He reached over and opened the door for her. "I'll call you when I've got the marriage ceremony organized; you get hold of your doctor, Red, and let me know the time and place."

He left her standing in the driveway as he backed up. She shivered suddenly in the semidarkness. The house— her home—had welcoming lights within. Leigh knew Robert would have prepared dinner in her absence. All she had to do was walk in there and she'd be enveloped in the soothing folds of familiar domesticity—of Robert and dinner and washing up her favorite hand-painted china, of the work she'd brought home from White's for the weekend. She worked overtime from choice rather than need—she liked the anonymous facts and statistics that required all her concentration.

Yet she turned away from the lamplit windows to stare into the darkness where the Morgan had disappeared. She was out of Brian's mind, she was sure. His dinner engagement no doubt involved a woman, and it did not take an extraordinary amount of perceptiveness to figure out that the woman wouldn't be the type to hold hands in a museum, or to go all prudish and adolescent over a few kisses. Leigh could well imagine the kind of women Brian dated: elite women, the country-club set. Leigh had grown up with them. Hardly hand-holders, she thought wryly. One had to worry about appearances, and one's hairdo and one's makeup—at least until the evening was over and the lights were out, and such things no longer mattered. Cats' eyes all looked the same in the dark, her stepfather had said once.

That had been the beginning, when Leigh had first started to hate David Hines. He had spoken in front of her mother that time, but his narrow eyes had been focused suggestively on Leigh. Andrea had found it amusing that her daughter had been so upset. Of course David was looking at her, she'd said later; Leigh had a lovely figure, didn't she? A lot of men were going to look at her that way. "You'll learn to love it, darling," she'd concluded with a smile.

"But he's your husband," Leigh had blurted out, a very young and naïve sixteen.

"He's a man," Andrea had retorted. "And don't you forget—they're all the same in the dark, too."

Leigh had been shocked by her mother's cynicism. But there had come a time when she had been forced to believe her. Men *were* all alike. Leigh had tried, but she could never be the kind of woman her mother so admired—hard and invulnerable and cold, using her sexuality to get what she wanted from life. Leigh could deal with her fears far better than she could shut off her heart from all feeling, the way Andrea had done.

I have to trust you, Brian, she thought fleetingly, but only a moment later she thought that what she really trusted was his willingness to surround himself with anonymous tiger eyes in the night.

Chapter 5

LEIGH'S HANDS WERE clenched tightly in her lap as she stared unseeingly at the series of brightly colored posters on the walls of the doctor's office. Brian, next to her, hadn't said one word from the time he had entered the office and taken the nearest chair to her. His face was impassive as a statue's, but already she was too sensitive to him not to guess how he felt: He disliked everything about this; and he disliked Leigh for putting him through it.

Determinedly she tried to concentrate solely on babies, on the possible look, feel, touch, and smell of the child she wanted so badly. The child was possible only because she was here, and for one minute she felt sheer exhilarating hope, but then came the dampening awareness of the procedure that was soon to take place, and the more dampening awareness of the man next to her, so virile, so . . . still.

A white-clad nurse emerged from the inner office and beckoned. Leigh stood up, trying with moist palms to shift her purse strap to her shoulder. It slipped and she flushed, following the nurse with awkward steps, aware of Brian's stare on her back.

"I want you to relax now, honey," the nurse told her some fifteen minutes later. "That's absolutely all you have to do."

It seemed a century later that she was walking back out to the waiting room, making her way through a sea of faces to the receptionist's desk. Her knees were shaky and her face chalk white. The receptionist told her the amount of the bill, and Leigh stared at her blankly. Kindly, the receptionist repeated it.

"Pardon? Oh, yes, I . . ." They were all kind. She'd suffered no pain, but it was exactly as Brian had said: terribly impersonal, embarrassing, and clinical. But it would be all right once she could concentrate on the baby again. It was just that she couldn't seem to think of the baby at that moment—only of the cold, clinical procedure and how incredibly different it might all have been if not for that nightmare eight years ago . . .

Damp fingers fumbled with her handbag, and to her embarrassment the change purse slipped and coins clattered noisily to the floor. Her eyes widened when she felt Brian's hand, firm and sure, on her shoulder. He bent to pick up the coins, took the purse from her trembling fingers. She'd thought he would be gone; there was no reason for him to wait, and they had come in separate cars. The tightness in his posture she had noticed earlier was gone, but his face was still a cold mask. He neither looked at her nor she at him as she finally managed to pay, but his palm still rested supportively on the small of her back as he ushered her from the doctor's office.

"I'm driving you home; I'll have someone pick up your car later," he said as they walked the distance to the parking lot, his arm still firmly gripping her waist.

"There's absolutely no need. I'll—"

"Shut up, Red."

Tears fell silently all the way home as she huddled near the passenger door, mortified that she could not control herself, that he ignored her completely. In the driveway, Brian dispassionately took out a handkerchief and dried her tears. She felt too weak, inside and out, to stop him. It was so ironic that yesterday she had gotten through the twenty-minute wedding at the courthouse with flying colors, while today she was falling apart. The thought of marriage should have been what upset her. Today they were making a baby, and she had no reason at all to cry.

"Leigh, was it so painful?" he asked quietly as he dropped the handkerchief and almost absently brushed a copper strand of hair from her cheek. "Does it hurt now?"

"No." She shook her head, feeling the insane urge to press her cheek to his palm. A shudder enveloped her body as she struggled to control yet another round of tears.

"Do I have to remind you that this is precisely how *you* wanted it?"

"But it *isn't* how I wanted it," she said passionately. "It's just that it was the *only* way! Leave it, Brian. I don't want to talk. I wish you hadn't waited."

Abruptly, he reached across her to open the car door. "I'll see you inside."

"No!" she protested. "Just leave me alone."

She saw the flash of anger in his eyes, but he let her go. She'd just taken a step toward the house when his own door opened. He stood up, staring at her over the hood of the car.

"For now, Leigh. For *now*, I'm leaving, but I understand you can take the first test in three weeks. Don't be so foolish as to leave me waiting longer than a month."

She nodded in automatic agreement, a vague motion of her head. She was aware that he watched her silently until she had safely traveled the distance to the front door and made her way in. By an act of will, she put him out of her mind as soon as she was safely inside her home. He was her husband. His essence of love and life was already inside of her. She was not going to think of either. Or of the nightmares.

Two days passed, and then three weeks more, while Leigh filled her days with work, grateful for the concentration that the impersonal facts and figures of her job demanded. She put Brian and babies out of her mind, filling every waking hour with activities designed to cushion her expectations and desperate hopes.

She took the first pregnancy test at the soonest possible moment, on a Monday morning. It was positive, she was told on Tuesday.

Her mood changed abruptly. Driving from the doctor's office, she found herself laughing out loud with sheer, uninhibited joy. At home, she canceled all appointments, filled the house with flowers, went out and spent a ridiculous amount of money on groceries for dinner—and sent a box of the most expensive cigars she could find to Brian's office, anonymously. And then she promptly forgot him altogether, as she had for the last three weeks. He could do as he liked; what did she care? Somewhere he had a piece of paper that proclaimed her last name was Hathaway, but if he had changed his mind in the last few weeks she would not press him. She had her baby! Her whole afternoon rolled around the wonder of it, a feeling of love growing inside her, a bubble that could not be burst.

Dinner was a real occasion. To Robert's consternation, she had forced him into an old sport jacket that he hadn't worn in fifteen years, and Leigh dressed herself in a long skirt of ice-blue velvet with a matching top. Candles had been placed on the table, and the menu, according to Robert, was not to be believed: fresh lobster, out of season; fresh strawberries, out of season; fresh asparagus, out of season; and champagne.

"Would you mind telling me what we're celebrating?"

"Can't we just celebrate?" she suggested impishly.

"You know," the old man said perceptively, "you look like the cat that swallowed the canary. I've never seen you react to your job with quite that sort of color in your cheeks before."

"I skipped work," Leigh admitted blithely. "Frankly, Robert, I called in sick and played hookey. I've never seen the leaves as beautiful as they are today; it seems as if they all turned at once this fall. And the chestnuts and walnuts are starting to fall."

"Leaving a godawful mess," Robert commented.

She chuckled, motioning his hovering figure away from the stove. "The asparagus will take about five more minutes," she said lightly. "During which time I could either sing 'Waltzing Matilda' or 'Good Night, Irene,' both of which I happen to know are your favorites."

"Honey, I do love you, but I shouldn't like to take the chance that your singing voice might curdle the champagne."

She laughed and looked at him fondly. In his old tweed jacket and bow tie, Robert had made every effort to look dapper for her nameless celebration. His face was so wrinkled that he could hardly tell where the bones were anymore, and he seemed more frail to her each day, with a slight tinge of blue around his lips that worried her terribly. Still, his mind was so clear and his tongue so sharp, and she really did love him dearly . . .

Suddenly, the doorbell rang. "Damn!" Leigh wailed. "Everything's just done, and it can't wait or it'll be spoiled!"

"I'll get it, I'll get it," Robert soothed her. "It's probably only that woman across the road still looking for her dog."

It took a while for Robert to negotiate the steps to the front door. She really should have gone herself, Leigh thought. And she was definitely going to insist that he take it easier around the house.

She opened the pot of asparagus, and steam clouded around her in fragrant puffs, bringing an instant flush to her cheeks. She nearly dropped the lid when she saw Brian standing there, with Robert behind him wearing a thoroughly satisfied grin.

"Just in time," the older man said happily.

"I didn't realize I'd be interrupting your dinner," Brian said, although Leigh thought he didn't sound the least bit apologetic.

"Don't be silly," Robert said hospitably. He was already getting additional cutlery from the drawer. "You're just in time to help us celebrate."

"Then Leigh told you . . . ?" Brian probed tactfully.

"All I know is that she's been dancing around all day," Robert said with his customary gruffness. "Now you're here, maybe you can tell me what it's all about."

Leigh continued to fuss with serving dishes and pots, but her heart was thundering in her chest. Inevitably, she had to look up, and Brian's eyes seemed to be just waiting to catch hers. She felt like a fool for sending him the cigars; a brief note would have been the sensible thing. She was embarrassed, and felt an odd stillness curling inside the longer he studied her. His broad chest blocked out Robert's image, so it almost seemed as if only the two of them were there. His eyes skimmed all of her, the flowing mass of copper hair and the sparkling topaz eyes, the soft lips vulnerably parted, the sensual lines of her figure accented by the long, graceful skirt. She felt a quiver of uncertainty inside. He hadn't looked at her like that before.

Relaxed, sure of himself, Brian leaned back against the door while she continued to work. "What's for dinner?" he asked finally.

She told him.

"Oh," he said dryly.

There was a wealth of meaning in that word, she mused, thinking that she should resent the stereotype of the newly pregnant woman with strange cravings; but she didn't. She flashed him a private smile. He knew how much this meant to her, and she didn't really care what he or anyone thought of her dinner.

"You don't have to stand on ceremony for me, you know," Robert told Brian bluntly.

"Stand on ceremony?"

The matchmaker nodded. "I know you haven't had a chance to see Leigh in a few weeks. I told her all along I knew there was something between you. Maybe you two do things differently than in my day, but if it needs saying, I wouldn't be shocked out of my mind if you . . . well, you know."

"I get the drift," Brian said blandly. So did Leigh, staring at Brian with startled eyes as he came closer. She put the platter of lobster between them, which he just as quickly removed to the table, his black eyes noting her distress with amusement. It was all happening just a little too quickly. Of course, for Robert's sake there would eventually have to be some token gestures of affection, but not this moment, not before she had a chance to steel herself.

His mouth dipped to hers, a strong, firm palm nestling at the back of her head. He tasted first, his eyes boring so intensely into hers that she helplessly closed her own, her whole body rigid with panic. He tasted again, this time lingering, and then his mouth simply covered hers, stealing

the breath from her as his tongue parted her lips. She tried
to remember Robert's presence, her pride. Her arms seemed
to be in midair, a spoon in one hand. She could feel his
erratic heartbeat on top of her own, the foreign sensation
of her breasts intimately crushed, pressed deliberately against
the solid, ungiving wall of his chest. For just an instant,
she had a wild, crazy feeling...

Slowly, Brian released her, his palms trailing down her
sides to her waist before he let her go. He was watching
her. She took a deep breath with lowered eyes. "The ring
is about to go on Leigh's finger, Robert," Brian said conversationally.

"I should think so," the older man answered. The kiss
had clearly delighted him.

"I'll be moving in this weekend."

Momentarily, Leigh felt stunned, as if she had just discovered herself to be barefoot outside in the snow. The kiss
was shiver material, but it was over. Brian's deep voice was
clearly saying he was taking possession, and in front of
Robert she would have to play along. She forced a smile
as she moved away from Brian and sat down at the table.

"Come on, both of you," she urged. She was starving;
she'd been dreaming of lobster for at least a week, and it
was a rare occasion when she had reason to chill champagne,
although she had intended the bubbly wine primarily for
Robert, contenting herself with the merest sip. She would
take no risk of jeopardizing the health of the baby growing
inside her.

"I saw your picture in the paper a few weeks ago," Robert
said pointedly to Brian. "Some blonde with you. A very
good-looking—"

"Don't worry about it, Robert," Leigh interrupted imperturbably. "I told him to have one last fling or I wouldn't
marry him." She hadn't lived with Robert for twenty-five
years without knowing that there was no point in trying to
silence him. He shot her a baleful glance, presumably to
silence *her,* then returned his eyes to Brian.

"Leigh and I were married three weeks ago," Brian said
quietly. "I suppose you're wondering about the timing, Robert, since I had to be away for the next three weeks. At the
time, I had in mind catching Leigh in a weak moment,

before she had the chance to change her mind. I know she didn't want to tell you until we could be together again."

Leigh dished out the strawberries, topping them with a dollop of whipped cream. Her own dish seemed to be the largest, she noticed, which was certainly very unhostesslike. Strawberries in October seemed to have an incredible appeal.

"No wonder she's all dressed up to celebrate," Robert mused delightedly. "Well. More champagne, Brian! I had my suspicions, of course, and I approve of everything. Including your having the sense to take advantage of Leigh's 'weak moment.' She doesn't have many, you know. At least," the elderly man added with old-fashioned pride, "she isn't the type to run after a man."

"No one," Brian agreed ironically, "would accuse Leigh of that."

She took a breath, then spooned in a mouthful of strawberries. Brian was showing more understanding and kindness to Robert than she had ever expected, considering that he had walked in totally out of the blue. Robert was taken in like a four-year-old who believes in Santa Claus. Leigh was relieved that Robert was taking the big news so well, but it worried her to realize just how manipulative Brian was capable of being. She felt his eyes on her, but she didn't look up.

"In fact, it was certainly the opposite when she was a teenager," Robert continued. "The phone ringing all the time, every other night a different date. Not that she wasn't selective in her choices..."

"No," Brian agreed blandly.

"But none of them would have done, anyway. It was always going to take a strong man to handle Leigh, even then, I used to say to myself. And then, after all that business happened, of course she shut herself off for a while—"

"Robert!" The strangled cry of distress escaped involuntarily. Alertness was written all over Brian's face. She had never dreamed Robert would go so far.

"I'm sorry, Leigh." But Robert wasn't sorry; his look was clearly disapproving. "I shouldn't have brought it up. I assumed you would have told him, though.

"Some topics are not fit for discussion," she said tightly.

"Well, we won't discuss it then," Robert said agreeably. "The point was simply that it would take a strong man to chase away the nightmares. That was all I was going to say. A man who's any sort of man would make you forget all that nonsense."

"Is there any coffee?" Brian said abruptly, staring at Leigh intently.

She rose, unwillingly grateful that he had given her something to do, and unreasonably annoyed that he had so considerately changed the subject for her sake. She didn't want anything done for her sake—not by Brian, not by any man.

The coffee was poured, and when she sat back down at the table there was a tiny brown satin box in front of her place. She glanced up and saw Robert's beaming face. When she opened the box, she feared he looked so excited he was going to have apoplexy.

"Brian!" She'd told him she didn't want an engagement ring, and even if she had wanted one, she would never have expected anything like this. The marquis diamond, surrounded by sapphires, flamed mysteriously in the candlelight. The setting was delicate and of very old gold, simple in design yet exquisite. "It's beautiful," she said quietly, looking up at him unhappily. His next words made her feel even worse.

"The stones were my mother's. I had them reset in a style I thought you'd like. Shall I put it on for you?"

"No!" Reluctantly, she slipped the ring on, not wanting his hand to touch hers. When she looked at him again, there was a glint of . . . something in his eyes. He had won, of course. She was wearing the ring.

"I also brought the wedding rings," Brian continued, unruffled, as he withdrew another box containing the plain gold bands that Leigh had thought would be the only token of their marriage.

"Well, if you two will excuse me, I think I've had all the excitement I can handle for one evening."

"Oh, Robert, I . . ." A moment ago, she would have been happy to see Robert fade into the woodwork, but then she hadn't had the chance to consider that his absence would put her alone with Brian. She was suddenly unsure of him: the kiss, the tactful consideration of Robert, the engagement

ring. Her trust in the man who was now her husband was
tenuous at best, and she hoped he had no other surprises in
store for her.

"Good night, Robert," Brian said firmly.

Chapter 6

As soon as Robert was gone, Leigh rose to set the dessert dishes on the counter and bring the coffeepot back to the table. She poured both cups before she sat down again, and then simply looked at Brian. Really looked at him.

They had eaten by candlelight; it would have been awkward to change the arrangement when Brian arrived, and Leigh loved the softness of candles. There were a half-dozen ribbons of flame, all of which accented his masculinity. He looked broader, larger, in the semidarkness. His black eyes reflected tiny fires; the hollows beneath his cheekbones were shadowed. The humor had left his face, which seemed now to have no expression at all, just an aura of strength and brooding silence.

Leigh felt agitated. He was right there, the cold-blooded, always-in-control man with a gift for manipulating people, the man she had married because she believed he'd never give a damn about her. Still, if she closed her eyes for only a few seconds and opened them again, she seemed to see another Brian: the father of her child, a man capable of sensitivity and understanding, iron-willed, but . . . human. In the candlelight she could see the dark circles under his eyes, the little lines of fatigue on his face.

"Brian, you look exhausted," she said gently, as the wariness she'd been feeling faded somewhat.

His eyes flickered to hers, filled with annoyance. "I am." It was obvious to Leigh that he didn't appreciate her noticing the chink in his armor.

"Why don't you relax in the living room for a few minutes, while I get the dishes done," she suggested.

"Leigh, are you absolutely sure?" he asked abruptly. "It's only been three weeks."

"If the test had been negative, it wouldn't have been positive this early. But since it was positive, it was positive!"

"I dare you to repeat that."

She smiled. "I'm sure," she said simply.

"You got what you wanted."

Leigh nodded, seeing it in exactly those terms: She had everything she wanted. It seemed so much more than he could possibly get out of their bargain. "How's Joan?" she asked idly, referring to the woman he'd been with in the newspaper photo that had upset Robert.

"Would you really like to know?" He poured himself a second cup of coffee and settled back into the chair at the head of the table.

"Not if you feel it's prying. But yes, I would really like to know." Particularly if that would erase the lines of exhaustion around his eyes. She didn't care about him, of course, but it was odd, having pictured Brian as someone invincible, someone too damned hard and strong to be hurt, and then seeing that he had problems and tensions of his own.

"Four nights in a row I've been working late, on that college project I mentioned to you. Anyway, I didn't get home last night until midnight, and when I got in, Joan was there. The daughter of the 'dean to be,'" he added dryly. "The door was locked and she didn't have a key, but she claimed the night watchman let her in. She had on a robe of mine, and nothing else. I know, because she took off the robe as soon as I got my coat off."

Leigh leaned forward. "I get your point," she said stiffly, "now kindly listen to mine. No, I really don't care about your evening with Joan, or with Sue, Mary Jane, or whomever. But you looked tired as hell, Brian, and I was just trying to tell you that there's no reason for you to worry if some woman's name does slip out in conversation, that you don't have to feel any awkwardness just because you're leading your own life." She sighed at his cryptic expression. He was impossible to read. "Look, if the arrangement doesn't suit you, you're not tied to it. Any time you want out, we can get divorced."

Abruptly, he stood up. "I don't want out. And I don't understand you, Red," he said tersely.

For a moment, she felt wary again, catching a flash of anger on his face that was just as quickly masked. "That really doesn't matter, does it?" she said swiftly.

"We'll see."

He left the kitchen, and Leigh turned back to the dishes. She spent a half hour puttering around cleaning up. When she finally went into the living room, she found the lights still off and the room empty. She found him in the library, and was amused to see that he had fallen asleep in the recliner chair. It was the room she'd expected he would lay claim to; with its dark paneling and books and large, overstuffed chairs, it was the most masculine room in the house.

For a moment she debated waking him, and then thought better of it. She could wake him in the morning, in time for him to go home and change clothes before work. She was always an early riser, and if he got up in the middle of the night he could certainly find his own way out. He'd already removed his shoes, and he didn't so much as stir when she placed an afghan over him. She left a small light burning, because it didn't seem right to let him waken suddenly in a strange room in the dark. And then she left him.

"Robert, would you just leave it alone? I feel perfectly wonderful today!" Absently, Leigh glanced out the dining room window at a bleak November afternoon that threatened snow, thinking what a violent change in weather they'd undergone in the last month.

"Just answer my question; *then* I'll leave you alone," Robert retorted. He had a deck of cards on the dining table, spread out for a game of solitaire. Leigh could tell from the way he stopped every so often that his arthritis was bothering him today, but there was no point in suggesting he put an end to the game. Robert invariably wiled away the hour before dinner with cards, and it was a habit he rarely broke.

"You're cheating," she pointed out.

"The card slipped," corrected Robert, giving her an injured look.

She chuckled, knowing very well that the "slip" had been intentional.

"Well?" he continued. "Are you having the nightmares again? Is that why I hear you pacing at night?"

"No, I am *not* having nightmares. Would you please stop worrying about me, Robert!"

"Are you sick with the baby then? Or are you pacing the floor because Brian's out so much? You know, Leigh, I don't think much of these modern marriages, when the couples just seem to go their own ways. Brian's been living here a month, but you hardly see him any more than I do. I'm not one to criticize . . ."

"Since when?" teased Leigh.

He harumphed in exasperation, set his mouth tightly, and turned his attention back to the cards. Guiltily, Leigh sighed. "Honestly, Robert, I'm perfectly okay. It's just a little bout of insomnia, nothing at all to worry about."

"For a man in his eighties, insomnia is nothing to worry about," Robert answered stubbornly.

But he left it at that, for which Leigh was grateful. Nausea engulfed her again, forcing her to lean against the counter momentarily. This day was the worst she'd had in a long time, compounded by several nights of unrelieved nausea and sleeplessness. The idea of eating dinner was appalling, but at least Brian wouldn't be there. And Robert was just as pleased as she was to have a light supper of soup and scrambled eggs; simple meals seemed to suit his digestion best.

Later Leigh made a fire in the living-room fireplace, all for herself to savor and enjoy. Over the past month, she had removed her mother's formal French Provincial furniture to the attic, and had redecorated the room in a style of her own choosing. Two massive burnt-orange couches in a tufted corduroy velvet now occupied the middle of it. A massive oak trunk stood between them, a treasure Leigh had unearthed from an antique shop to refinish and use as a coffee table. In front of the fireplace were two nut-brown chairs sufficiently large for Leigh to curl up in, and comfortable enough to elicit an automatic sigh of relaxation from Brian when he sank down in one, on one of the rare evenings he was home. The richly stuccoed walls had been freshly painted in cream.

With the exception of this room, nothing seemed to be working out quite as she had expected. She had anticipated a delightful nine months of being pregnant. After all, she was healthy, happy, and more secure than she had ever been in her life. Yet here she was, less than two months into the pregnancy, and it was not going well. Morning sickness—only it didn't hit her just in the morning. Sometimes, yes, but more often the nausea would attack her at night, waking her from a sound sleep. She couldn't seem to keep anything down. She craved food, devoured huge meals as if she were starving, and then just as quickly lost them. She'd had to take a leave of absence from her job, so she could sleep during the day after a restless night.

The marriage, on the other hand, was going a lot better than she could ever have imagined. Brian was so rarely around, for one thing. A few nights a week he would call to say he would make it home for dinner, and those meals inevitably passed pleasantly. Of course Robert was always there. But Brian also had a dry sense of humor that she'd discovered she liked; in a very quiet way, he made her feel appreciated when she put extra effort into a dinner, and he made very few demands of any kind on the household. The evenings he was home he invariably shut himself up in the library with his work, and Leigh was left entirely in peace. Brian actually seemed to seek from marriage exactly those things he'd said he wanted—peace and quiet—a haven of sorts for a very busy man. Not to mention an escape hatch from any overly ardent lady friends.

Leigh heard the ticking of the chime clock and closed

her eyes, delighted that for once her stomach was calm. She rose after a time and stoked the fire, adding a few more cherry logs. Sparks splashed the brick walls of the fireplace, and tufts of smoke soared up the chimney. When the flames simmered down again, she settled back in the deep cushions of the fireside chair and drew her feet up under her.

Again she reflected how very different Brian was from the man she'd originally thought him to be. It wasn't that they hadn't had a few...skirmishes, she recalled with amusement. She knew, for instance, without his ever having said a word, that he did not like whitefish, her hair up, his papers in the library touched, the color purple, or cheese sauce on broccoli.

There had been a little verbal warfare in other arenas too. When Robert had told him she was redoing the living room, Brian had hired an unasked for and unwanted trio of painters. When Robert mentioned Leigh's gardening chores, she suddenly found a man outside one day, raking leaves she was perfectly capable of raking herself. And when Robert tattled that Leigh had a woman come in once a week to do the heavy cleaning, that woman mysteriously began coming twice a week instead.

All of which had gone to prove, she thought wryly, that Robert was a terrible bearer of tales, and that Brian was not the self-absorbed egotist she'd once thought him. She didn't like or appreciate his consideration—she didn't want anything from Brian—but it was impossible not to admit that her trust in him had grown. He hadn't touched her, beyond a casual kiss or two in front of Robert. And that wasn't so awful, just simple affection. He was so strangely gentle with her...

She leaned her head back wearily, more content than she had felt in years.

Later, much later, she pulled the comforter off her bed and threw her pillow on top of it, dragging them to the carpeted floor of the bathroom. It was only eleven, but she had already been in bed for an hour, with a bone-tired weariness that she had been certain would overrule her stomach this night. But the room had started to spin and the nausea churn almost the minute her head touched the pillow.

She was just so discouraged, and though the doctor had told her the nausea was normal and would disappear after the third month had passed, that meant there was still more than a month to go!

Another spasm of nausea wrenched through her and she leaned miserably over the basin, brushing her teeth thoroughly afterward and settling back on her makeshift pallet on the floor. There was no point in going back to bed; it was just as warm on the carpeted floor, or almost, and at least she wouldn't have to keep dashing between bed and bathroom.

The next time, she was awakened from a sound sleep and had to lean both arms on the counter of the basin to support her weakened body. The awful retching just wouldn't stop, though there was nothing left inside her stomach by that time. The dry heaves continued, horrible and exhausting. And then suddenly she felt a strong arm under her breasts, holding her up, startling her half out of her mind.

"Oh, God! Go away!" she cried to Brian. And still the nausea overwhelmed her, choking off her protest. Finally, it passed. Leigh was shaking so violently she could barely stand up. "Go away, please, Brian," she pleaded, loath to have him see her like this. Tears welled in her eyes, tears of weakness and humiliation, and she combed his fingers from around her stomach, frantically pushing them away. Without a word, he picked the comforter up from the floor and cradled it around her while she brushed her teeth, and when she set the toothbrush down, he picked her up in one deft movement, comforter and all.

Tears streamed uncontrollably down her cheeks. "What are you doing here?" she said between sobs.

He sat down on the edge of the bed and pulled her onto his lap as if she were a child, crooning something incomprehensible to her, something soothing and soft. The flood of tears spilled all over his shirtfront. "I'm sorry, I'm sorry," she tried to say. She couldn't remember ever feeling so miserable. The discouragement, the tiredness, the nausea, the humiliation—it was all too much.

"It's all right, Leigh," he soothed. Cradling her in his arms, he rocked her back and forth as he would rock a frightened child, one hand gently smoothing the tousled hair back from her forehead. For endless minutes he held her like that, until the sobs subsided and she took several deep breaths, fighting for control. In some dim corner of her mind she was aware of how strange it felt to have his arms around her. She hated and resented the feeling of dependence . . . but for just this moment, this single moment, the hard steel of his body did not seem at all threatening, and the sensual, gentle strength of his fingers reaching out to her was a luxury she simply couldn't deny herself.

Finally she brought her hands to her face and wiped away the tears. "Lord, I'm sorry," she repeated shakily. "I'm so embarrassed; it's just that so much has been wrong lately."

"Tell me," he suggested. She lifted her eyes, suddenly aware of how close his face was to hers. She was conscious of the smooth texture of his mouth and his emotive black eyes, the sensual smell of him, the power she felt in his thighs beneath hers. A stark burst of sheer sexuality flamed inside her, immediately accompanied by a quelling panic. She tried to get up from his lap, and his arms encircled her like iron. "Just tell me first," he said.

"It's all so foolish," she admitted unhappily, staring at the damp folds of his shirt where she had cried so easily. Confused, she confessed to him all that had been happening: She couldn't get anything done because she was so tired during the day; she was tired during the day because she was ill at night; she couldn't keep any food down; she had no energy, and she had always had so much energy; and she cried for no reason at all . . . and she never cried. "I don't have any reason to cry. I've never been so happy, Brian, and everything is perfectly wonderful. None of it makes any sense."

"Of course it does, sweetheart. You're pregnant," Brian said gently. "Now will you be all right if I leave you for a few minutes?" Still he cradled her in his arms as he got up, and then propped the pillow against the headboard and laid her head on it. Startled, she watched his right hand as if it were some strange independent being, the fingers tugged down the nightgown that had ridden to her thighs, pulled the sheet back up to her waist and folded it just under her breasts. His palm rested momentarily on her ribs, warm and firm, then slid down her stomach, hovered a moment on her covered thigh. "I'll be right back." His black eyes seared hers. "Anything wrong, Red?"

"No." She closed her eyes, unwilling to reveal how much his touch disturbed her. A few minutes later, Brian returned with a tray. She almost laughed when she saw it. Ginger ale and soda crackers. "I couldn't, Brian, honestly. Really, you don't have to bother anymore. I'm all right now."

He brought back the second pillow from the bathroom and, placing it next to hers on the double bed, settled himself down beside her. It was crazy. He was still dressed in his suit pants and his white and now thoroughly rumpled shirt; she wore a long cream-colored flannel nightgown... together, next to each other on the bed. She closed her eyes, willing her childish panic to evaporate. It just wasn't that kind of moment; the scene he'd just witnessed could not possibly evoke desire. She was safe with him, had felt safe for a month.

"It is rather wicked, isn't it?" he said devilishly, and when her eyes widened he said calmly, "Eating crackers in bed. You'll probably toss on crumbs for the rest of the night."

She chuckled. The crackers tasted absolutely delicious. The sense of weakness passed with each bite. "Robert tattled, didn't he?" she asked sharply.

"Why didn't *you* tell me?"

"Obviously because I didn't want you to know," she said frankly. "The pregnancy isn't your problem, Brian. I mean, our arrangement's been going very well, don't you think? I have no intention of bothering you again—I'm not normally that sick."

"It bothers the devil out of you to have to admit you might actually need someone, doesn't it? It bothers you so much that you *won't* admit it, even now!"

"I don't need anyone," Leigh said stiffly. "I told you I was perfectly capable of coping on my own."

"The hell you are! Sleeping on the bathroom floor, overextending yourself with massive projects like painting rooms, gorging yourself one minute and starving the next! You've been coping just splendidly!" His arms folded behind his head in a relaxed manner, Brian managed to convey amusement as well as sternness. "Lady, you're about to be taken in hand."

He was deliberately confusing her. She was outraged that he should even imply that he had a right to influence her lifestyle, and amazed that he would want to. Although her pregnancy hadn't been going well, she had at least thought their marriage had been—that their relationship suited him as well as it did her. "I don't need anyone to hold my hand and I never will," she snapped furiously. "And I don't know what you think you're thinking of, Brian, but you can't very well stay home nights. Whatever women you're seeing are hardly going to just sit at home doing needlework while you baby-sit a pregnant wife!"

"My horde of mistresses you comfort yourself with?" he asked dryly. "Would you like a legal pad full of names, Leigh? Would that make you feel nice and safe?"

His candor shocked her. He had never raised his voice in her presence, yet she understood, in a moment, the difference between the kid-gloves quiet he had treated her with over the last month and the dangerous quiet he was capable of in other circumstances. It was all more than she could handle just now, and she pulled back the comforter to get out of bed.

"Where do you think you're going?"

"To the kitchen," she answered flatly. "I'm starving."

"No, you're not." But he had not moved, and she ignored him. Where was her robe? She usually put it on the chair next to her bed, but it wasn't there and it didn't seem to be in the closet. There, it had been buried in the fallen spread on the floor.

"Button up," he said shortly.

Startled, she looked at Brian and then followed the direction of his eyes. The cream-colored flannel nightgown was fully figure-concealing—when it was all buttoned up. She had no idea when the buttons had slipped loose, but one ripe, swollen breast was all but pouting at him, and an insanely long expanse of soft white skin was exposed nearly to the navel. Her long hair swirled around her flaming cheeks as her fingers fumbled at the buttons. "Oh...I..." Good Lord, how long had she been exposed like that?

"A long time, Leigh." Brian read her thoughts. "I waited to tell you because I wanted to make a point."

"Which is?" she demanded frostily.

"That the mere sight of a woman's breast is not an automatic stimulus to rape." His words sank in slowly and brought a renewed flush to Leigh's cheeks. Had her fears really been so transparent? "Now, if you put that robe back on, I'm going to take it off. You are *not* going to the kitchen for a midnight meal. The idea is to never let your stomach get too empty—*or* too full—or haven't you had the sense to speak to the doctor yet?"

"Of course I have! Stop talking to me as if I were two years old!" Defiantly, she slipped into the robe, taking a very long time with the buttons and sash.

"Take it off," he ordered ominously.

"You're right. I won't go down to the kitchen," she acceded quickly. But the robe was suddenly protection against a chill that was almost making her tremble. She could no more have stepped a foot closer to the bed with Brian lying there than she could have flown. Everything, suddenly, was very different than it had been a half hour before.

"Take it off and get back into bed," he repeated.

"Look," she started furiously, but one glance at his stony face silenced her. She took off the robe and awkwardly dove under the covers, staying so close to the edge of the bed that she practically fell off. "You're frightening me," she accused him pleadingly.

"I've had quite enough of that, too, Red," he said with annoyance. He stood up, and with hands on hips studied her. "Don't lay a guilt trip on me, because I won't accept it. I have no intention of vanishing into thin air just because you claim you're frightened. As I said," he repeated, striding around to her side of the bed, "it's time you were taken in hand." He reached out, ignoring her cringing, and quietly smoothed the covers under her chin, tucking them around her like the most efficient of nursemaids. "Good night," he said curtly, and left her.

Chapter 7

THE NEXT MORNING brought the first snowfall of the year. Leigh did not make it downstairs until past nine o'clock, a thoroughly unusual occurrence. When she finally did wander into the kitchen, she was startled to find Brian sitting with Robert over coffee at the breakfast table, and a pile of envelopes at the place where Leigh always sat.

"What's going on?" she asked warily. To her knowledge, Brian never left the house later than seven in the morning. "And what's this?" She pointed to the stack of envelopes.

"Invitations," Brian answered absently. "I think it's time you got out of this house, Leigh. Pick no more than two a week, and let me know the dates and times."

"But what are they for?" Robert placed a small bowl of cereal and a plate of toast in front of her, and that was even more bewildering. "And what do you think you're doing, waiting on me?" she scolded him.

"I don't want to go to any of these shindigs," Brian continued bluntly. "I happen to like the drawing-board rather than the bar side of business, and Taylor and Mike are usually pretty good about keeping the social load off my back. But they can't do all of the partying with the holidays coming on. I've been to a few of these affairs alone, not wanting to add to your burdens, but people think it's pretty damn peculiar for a newly married man to show up solo."

He actually made it sound as if she'd been remiss in her "wifely" duties. Robert was looking at her chidingly. "Brian," she said crisply, "I thought we discussed this after our marriage was announced in all the gossip columns. We agreed that except for a few celebrations with close friends, and the trip to your mother's at Christmas, we weren't going to alter our respective social lives." It was difficult to speak openly with Robert right there. "Now, if my presence at certain functions is required for business reasons, that's one thing. But I didn't expect you'd try to turn me into some kind of social butterfly."

"Do you turn into a leper when you step outside the house?" Brian's eyebrows arched in innocent curiosity.

"I thought you preferred *other* company for social outings," she hissed pointedly.

"What on earth does she mean by that, Robert?"

Robert was obligingly mystified. "I haven't the least idea. She's very good at entertaining, you know. The house used to be filled with people seven days a week when her mother was alive, and Mr. Hines. Everyone always said that Leigh had the gift of making people comfortable."

"Robert, I am *not* looking for brownie points from you this morning!" And then Leigh glared at Brian. His social and sex lives were separate from their home life, by his choice as well as hers. Not that she would mind attending an occasional business dinner or cocktail party, but . . . "I really haven't any clothes for that sort of thing."

"If you're done with your breakfast, we're about to take care of that," Brian said imperturbably. He finished his coffee, set the cup on the counter, and leaned an arm against the doorjamb, plainly waiting.

She shook her head in bewilderment. "What about your work?"

"The place won't crumble if I skip out a few hours. I've already called to say I'll be in late today."

"But what if I get ill?"

"We'll cope with that, Red," he said patiently. "You had a moderate breakfast and you're not going to get worn out; I'll see to that. The fresh air should do you good."

"All right." Her lips tightened. "I'll go shopping then. But there's no need for you to go with me. In fact, I can't think of anything more ridiculous than you in a women's clothing store, sitting there patiently while I try on dresses."

"I can't either," he admitted dryly. "I can't think of anything worse."

"Well, then?"

"You have an eye for color, Red, but not for style," he said critically. "If a dress doesn't choke you at the neck with buttons, it's got an extra yard of material there, or else you just don't own it." Robert chortled with suppressed laughter.

"I buy what I like."

"Which is why you're not buying anything. *I* am. Now say good-bye to Robert, Leigh. And put the spoon down. There hasn't been anything in that cereal bowl for at least five minutes."

Leigh said good-bye to a beaming Robert, with every intention of exploding over Brian's patronizing attitude the moment they were alone. But she did not argue with him once they got in the car. The fresh snow made the roads hazardously slippery, and driving obviously required his full concentration. While they rode in silence, she all but forgot the morning's incident as she covertly studied Brian's impassive, strong-featured profile next to her.

If there had been no David Hines in her life, she might have wanted very much to pierce through Brian's layers of cool to the man she knew was beneath. Sometimes, when he was near her, the fear was blended with other emotions— an excitement within, an awareness of his physical strength and elemental maleness.

"Brooding, Leigh?" he asked quietly.

"No," she said quickly, temporizing, "I was thinking about my father."

"Were you close?"

She smiled. "Dad's whole world was his business. He loved finding a piece of property somewhere that no one wanted and turning it into a profitable venture. He died when I was ten, but I can still remember him. He wanted a son, I always knew that, and he was busy and didn't go in much for coddling. But he was there when I needed him." She hesitated. "When I was little, it seemed both of my parents had so many expectations; there was no possible way to live up to all of them, particularly when they each wanted different things for me. But before I ever got to the point of worrying, Dad would snatch me up, take me off somewhere for a day or even a week, just the two of us, and it was extra nice because I knew that I came first with him, before his business or anything else."

"Did you like your stepfather?"

It was impossible not to stiffen, and Brian was too perceptive not to notice.

"No," she answered shortly. They rode the rest of the way into Chicago in silence, Brian thoughtful and Leigh deliberately making her mind a blank.

When they arrived at the fashionable boutique Brian had chosen, he promptly told the saleswoman who greeted them that his wife was pregnant and required a chair. Then he went off with the woman and returned a while later laden with garments over his arms.

"Are you out of your mind?" Leigh whispered frantically. "I thought you meant for one or two dinners, and that you wanted to specify what sort of thing was appropriate."

"We need an office," Brian told the saleswoman, ignoring Leigh.

"We have dressing rooms..."

The owner of the shop had a pink and gilt office, complete with side bathroom and a powder-pink velvet loveseat. Apologizing for the disorder of her desk, she left with a smile. "I was pregnant myself once. Just make yourselves at home."

"Brian," Leigh said when the door was closed and every chair in sight piled high with garments, "you just don't do this. No one marches into a store and demands—"

He settled gingerly on the delicate loveseat, drew a folded newspaper from his pocket, and motioned her impatiently to the bathroom. "You mean taking over the owner's office? Why not?" There was a hint of a brusque smile when she rolled her eyes helplessly to the ceiling. "Leigh, the sales-women would have been hovering over you like vultures, telling you what to buy. This way, if you get tired, you can sit down. Just pick out a dozen or so and—"

"A *dozen?* One! Maybe two. *Maybe.*"

He refolded the newspaper, set one foot carefully on the coffee table, and managed to look bored. "To begin with, I don't want to have to go through all this again. And I hate to have to tell you, Red, but your present wardrobe isn't quite what you think it is. Those bulky tops you wear, for instance—you've even got a few that are getting outright tight. I don't see any sign of a tummy yet, but . . ." He grinned suddenly. "You'd better use the bathroom. God knows I've never seen a woman's body before."

"Oh . . . you . . ."

The insane thing was that she almost felt livid enough to strip in front of him. Almost. She took a handful of dresses and bolted for the bathroom, snapping on the light and momentarily staring at her face in the mirror. The panic of intimacy . . . Damnit, she wasn't some Victorian prude, some shy adolescent; he didn't understand. And how she *hated* that bland neutrality he put into his voice whenever he disapproved of something.

She shuffled rapidly through the garments, mindlessly choosing dresses she would never have chosen herself, with halter tops and V necks. It seemed that Brian had already considered her pregnancy; many of the gowns were empire style or fitted only subtly at the waist. For some reason, that made her all the more furious, and her hands reached unerringly for the first time in years to colors that accented her vibrant hair, her creamy skin, and to clinging fabrics that left little to the imagination.

When she finally emerged from the bathroom, she had a pile of garments on her arm designed specifically to break his bank, and her exasperation with him had not lessened. He took the clothes from her, giving only a moment's glance to her selections. "Good girl," he approved, with a speculative look at her flashing eyes, as if he would never have believed she had the taste to know what suited her.

With a sigh, she bit back the comment she would have liked to make, the explanation she—almost—wanted to give him. It startled her that even for a moment she could entertain the idea of actually confiding in him. She brushed the thought from her mind, knowing it would never be.

The shopping expedition marked a new era in their marriage. From then on, Brian came home from work every night. Most evenings, he retired into the library with his work, yet occasionally he would join Leigh in the living room with a book, sharing the opposite chair by the fire she inevitably made on these cold evenings.

She was no longer ill. She refused to be ill. The nausea was still part of her days, but the more carefully she moderated what she ate and drank, the better she felt.

She had finally come to the point where she talked easily to and felt comfortable with her husband—but only in front of Robert, and only when they discussed the sort of topics that made for light dinner conversation. She looked forward to these dinners, but was uneasy about Brian spending evening after evening with her. Leigh had the guilty feeling that he regarded her as an annoying responsibility, that he'd decided to take care of her because he thought she was too foolish to take care of herself. And yet he gave her no evidence to back up this suspicion. In fact, he seemed quite content with his newfound domesticity and even eager to show her off at the occasional party or dinner they attended. Leigh wondered what arrangements he had made with Joan and the other women in his life; perhaps he was now taking long lunch breaks at work to make time for his trysts. She wasn't about to ask, but she couldn't help thinking about it. And she couldn't help wondering nervously what other new directions their marriage might take.

Chapter 8

It was nearing seven when Leigh came down. Brian was waiting at the bottom of the stairs, dressed in a black cashmere sport jacket and pale gray pants, leafing through the sterling platter that held the day's mail. With his dark good looks accentuated, he struck Leigh as even more sophisticated and sensual than usual. He glanced up at the sound of her high heels on the parquet floor.

With an odd little pulse throbbing in her throat, she waited while he took in the very different look of her this evening. The cream-colored gown had medieval long sleeves and a deep V neck. Gold braid at the hem was accented by gold barrettes at the sides of her flowing auburn hair. She wore a subtle perfume that was new and softly feminine, and she had brushed on an array of makeup with a light but deliberate hand. The mirror had already told her that she looked radiantly lovely, and for just one instant in Brian's eyes . . .

"Very nice, Leigh," he said flatly, and turned away, busying himself with getting her coat from the closet.

The little pulse in her throat stilled. Did it matter so much that he saw her, just for once, as attractive? Perhaps even desirable? That thought started her pulse racing again, and she firmly banished it from her mind.

His voice was strangely harsh for no reason, as he held out her coat with his eyes averted. "Look, Red, I told you there's no reason for you to go to the Rawlings' with me. The other dinners were different—"

"Yes. You told me. And I told you that if you don't want me to go—"

"I told you it wasn't that," he said brusquely. "I just don't want to push you into something you can't handle. I told you what kind of man Steven Rawlings is."

"And also that you want to subcontract him for the electrical work on the college project," Leigh said in her best CPA voice. Brian opened the door and she stepped out to a night sky lazily tossing down snow. "And that he likes to do business socially, which is why we're going. He's good at his job, you want him, he specifically requested that you come with your wife, and I don't know why you keep bringing it up!"

"He's an ass," Brian said curtly. She wondered at the concerned frown he gave her as she slid into the car seat. The door shut with a bang, and Leigh nearly winced.

Their host-to-be wasn't an "ass." Brian had hinted very carefully at the kind of man he was: a womanizer. That Brian thought she couldn't handle the evening grated; his respect had become as essential to Leigh as her very breath. This was the fourth of their business evenings out, and she had felt that respect building as she handled his clients and colleagues with aplomb.

"I don't know how you got a reputation as a man-about-town," Leigh deliberately continued as Brian started the engine. "You seem to absolutely hate—"

"Drinking martinis one after the other. Wasting time with people I don't want to be with. I like business during business hours, that's all."

"It's only for one short evening!"

He glanced momentarily at her. *"You,* Red, keep that in mind."

The house was a sprawling example of contemporary architecture, standing bleak and cold in a treeless landscape. Leigh disliked it even before she stepped from the starry-soft night into the chrome glitter of the Rawlings' living room. And then, for a moment she felt her breath catch as their host made his way toward them. She'd met Steven Rawlings before, in an older version. Not tall, he had curly sandy hair and a practiced smile, and his blue eyes already had an alcoholic glaze as they focused almost leeringly on Leigh. "So you're Hathaway's lady, are you, darling? We understand congratulations are in order!"

He pressed a damp version of the European greeting on both her cheeks as his hands deliberately snaked their way up her torso to the sides of her breasts. Nausea burgeoned. She hadn't had the nightmare in months, but if he wasn't David Hines's son, he could have been.

"My wife, Janet . . ."

The blonde was kissing a hello to Brian. She wore a leather jumpsuit, designed to be worn over a shirt or sweater that she had apparently forgotten to put on. Her every movement revealed not just the curve of a stark white breast but its nipple as well. "Brian, honey, you haven't been to one of our parties in so long! I thought you'd forgotten all about us!" She turned with a distinctly cooler smile to Leigh, taking in her attire and looks. "Nice to meet you, Leigh. I hope you're going to help me keep our boys off business for at least a little while. I'm up for some fun tonight!"

Janet made manhattans for herself and Leigh and martinis for the men. The pair of long, tall pitchers would have served quite a crowd. The living room, in scarlet oak paneling, had been designed to imitate an English pub, and though Leigh found it attractive in its way, there was a strange absence of books and personal effects that might have made it warm.

"Leigh?"

She glanced at Brian, who had seated himself on one of three short sofas. Clearly, he was offering her the place next to him, but she didn't believe it was because he wanted her close. Smiling with deliberate vagueness, she stayed where she was, feeling like a feather in the wind. Still, she would handle the situation; she'd made it a long time without anyone's protection.

"Do you like modern art?" Janet questioned from behind the bar where she was getting herself a third drink. She motioned vaguely to the copper sculpture that stood on the coffee table in the midst of the couches. "I picked that up in Paris last year; I'm getting a pretty extensive collection if you like that sort of thing."

The copper man and woman were twisted in an explicitly erotic mode. Leigh wondered fleetingly if Janet collected pornography or modern art. "It's interesting," she said politely.

Janet grimaced. "Oh, well, you don't like it." She sighed and leaned back against the bar with a look of dissatisfaction as she listened for a moment to the business discussion Brian had initiated with her husband. "It looks like we'll have to do something to stir them up," she said lightly.

Quick as a cat, Janet curled up in the empty place next to Brian, with one long arm extended on the back of the couch so that her red-tipped fingernails rested languidly on his cashmere coat. She said something, leaning forward, giving him a clear glimpse of both breasts. In a moment, the two of them were laughing.

Leigh stepped forward with a smile that already ached from effort, set her glass down next to the contorted faces of the copper lovers, and sat on the scarlet velvet couch next to Steven Rawlings. If Brian was comfortable with these people, she was not going to let him see that she felt otherwise. With practiced ease, Steven drew an arm around her shoulders to hug her close. "I love newlyweds," he whispered teasingly. "They've always got just one thing on their minds. We don't believe in much formality around here, darling..."

Dinner was easier. At Brian's insistence, the two men did settle down to business, and Steven quickly changed into a model professional. He knew his electrical business and he talked it up well; in fact, he talked nearly all of the time. The contrast between the two men became more and more apparent to Leigh. Brian was a man the way her father had been a man. He didn't need to tell the world how strong and tough and good he was; he had nothing to prove. Steven, however, had something to prove every minute; her step-father had been of that same mold.

Thoughtfully, she raised the wineglass to her lips, suddenly catching Brian's eyes on her from across the table. He was still talking to Steven, but the intent look on his face made her uneasy. She had been quiet; was she failing him? At the other dinners they'd gone to she'd had the chance to ask questions and to listen, to encourage his clients to talk about themselves; there had been anecdotes, laughter. Tonight she felt out of her element, but if Brian expected something from her . . .

He did. She could see it in the haunting depths of his eyes. As if he were trying to tell her something, and no matter how she tried, she couldn't understand. He had the most beautiful eyes. Beautiful, dark, intimate eyes, eyes that touched her perfumed hair, and her nose and chin and slant of cheekbones, her lips . . . She found herself staring back almost wistfully, desperately trying to figure out what he wanted, so caught up in the black-fired depths that she could not look away.

"Come *on* now. Business is over and we've all had our coffee," Janet said petulantly. "I've got a new group of paintings I've been dying to show Brian, but first let's get some cognac from the living room." They all stood up at Janet's direction, Leigh lethargically feeling as if she were waking from a witch's spell. Janet was all vibrant sexual energy, winking at Leigh as if to say, I'm sure this is all right with you, as she wound an arm around Brian's waist.

"You two just go on then," Steven encouraged lazily. "Leigh and I will find some way to amuse ourselves."

"Perhaps Leigh would like to see—"

"Brian, Leigh doesn't like that sort of art," Janet scolded. "Surely you two have been married long enough to know her likes and dislikes? Or have you been spending all your time in bed?"

Leigh watched dispassionately as the two left the room. Inside she felt an unexpected jolt of panic at finding herself alone with another man. Brian had spelled protection for so long that she'd almost forgotten what that fear felt like.

"You like music, Leigh?" Steven's languorous appraisal of her figure suddenly became more personal, more threatening.

"Very much," she said softly.

"They'll be some time," he assured her. "The studio's an entirely separate building from the house."

She stood rather than sat once they moved into the other room. She couldn't deny that Steven had excellent taste in music or that his stereo was outstanding. But there was only so much time she could spend mulling over his eclectic record collection and exploring the curios in the room, and the minutes kept ticking by.

"You're very different than I thought you'd be. You're beautiful—of course. I expected that in Brian's mate. And you're remote, cool, yet also . . ." He smiled appreciatively at her, slouching on the couch with his legs extended. Leigh had the impression he'd tried the position before and knew it gave him an image of casual elegance. "Come on and sit by me," he coaxed, "while I try to think of the word to describe you." Abruptly, he snapped his fingers. *Demure.* That's the word I'm looking for. Demure, despite that flashy copper hair of yours. If you don't mind my saying so, it's sexy as all hell."

His words sounded so like a line that they almost had a boring ring to them. "Brian thinks so, too," she said pleasantly.

His eyebrow raised and a little of his smile faded. "We could find more amusing ways of spending our time than discussing what Brian thinks," he suggested.

Rather than roam a room she had already thoroughly roamed, she perched uneasily on the couch across from him, trying to look relaxed. "I envy you your music system, Steven. Have you had it long?"

He burst out laughing, but there was an annoyed look in his blue eyes. "Never let it be said that I can't take a hint," he said dryly.

More minutes went ticking by. Deliberately, Steven refused to initiate any conversation; an awkwardness settled in—in, around, all over.

"They've been gone a half hour now," Steven drawled finally.

She nodded. Long enough? Brian was a very sexual man—she'd never doubted that—who'd had to stay in a month of evenings because of her. Was that really how it was for him, a moment taken with a woman who was willing? Was that why he'd tried to talk her out of accompanying him tonight? "They have," she agreed quietly. "Your wife evidently has quite an extensive studio."

"Couch and all."

She reminded herself that Brian had to work with this man, and that she might have to dine with him again. "You seem to take a certain kind of pride in hinting at the . . . contemporary sort of marriage you have?" she queried carefully.

He mixed himself a drink, coming back to stand in front of her. "You want to talk about marriages, darling, let's talk about yours. Maybe that'll get your mind off the time," he grated, with a strange smile that held no warmth.

She smiled back with an aching jaw, and picked up the cup with her coffee in it. She didn't know whether all of his guests regularly switched partners with their hosts, but she could feel a dangerous thread of adrenaline in her bloodstream as he continued to stare at her suggestively. She was simply out of her depth. "I'd like to tell you about Brian and me," she managed calmly. "We have a sort of . . . contemporary marriage, too, you see. I don't know what he's doing at the moment, but I do know that it has nothing to do with our relationship."

His eyebrows flickered up sardonically. "You don't give a hoot in hell if he has sex on the side—and yet you're too pure to do likewise?"

His crudeness offended her. She had her back to the door as she raised the cup. "I'm just saying that there couldn't be anyone else but Brian for me."

"Well, I hate to have to tell you this, darling, but people just don't have marriages like that anymore. Miss Goody Two Shoes went out about a decade ago, haven't you heard? They used to say that men couldn't live without variety, but these days women, too, play that game every day."

"Yes," she agreed, and again reminded herself that Brian wanted to do business with this man. She knew that if she'd been the least approachable Steven would have made a pass, and she knew exactly what he thought Janet and Brian were doing. She had not felt so desolate in a long time. Yet pride urged her to prove she could handle the man—perhaps not well, perhaps not at all well—but at least to the extent that there was no question in his mind of where she stood. The words came of their own volition. "Yes," she repeated, "and I told you we have a very contemporary relationship—based on no one's standards but our own. I know what Brian brings to me. I just can't imagine wanting anyone else. But if he does want someone else, on occasion, and as long as it doesn't take anything away from what he brings to me . . ." She shrugged expressively.

"A very unusual attitude," Steven said sarcastically.

"Very unusual," Brian agreed dryly. His voice was less than three feet behind her. She refused to turn around and look at him. How long had he been standing there? How much had he overheard?

"Your wife's been telling me about your prowess as a lover," Steven supplied lazily, his composure never lost. Leigh stared disbelievingly at him.

"Someday I'll tell you about her prowess as a conversationalist. Right now we're going home." A strong hand grasped hers, drawing her to a standing position. Where was Janet? "Terrific dinner, Steven, and I'll see you again as soon as the attorney has a chance to draw up the contract. Be nice to work with you again."

Casual, normal words continued between the two men while coats were fetched and put on. Brian buttoned Leigh's with none of the patience he showed in his conversation, and almost roughly pushed her out the door ahead of him. On the brightly lit porch, with a gentle snow falling around them, Brian paused and grasped her shoulders. She looked up at him, frightened and wary and totally mute. She assumed he was angry, the way his eyes blazed into hers, and then for an instant she thought it wasn't anger at all, but frustration and . . . something else.

The moment was broken. "That damned woman! And damn Rawlings, too." With his hand imprisoning hers, he half-dragged her to the car with long, swift strides. He opened her door and slammed it once she was inside. When he got in, he was hardly seated before he had turned the key in the ignition and backed out of the driveway.

"And am I also on your list of the damned?" she inquired, wondering at his fury. "Or are you just taking your anger at them out on me?"

"Red, you have one hell of a nerve," he said with a short, impatient laugh that made her shiver inside.

Leigh sensed, from the deepest recesses of her mind, too many things that she was not sure she wanted to know: that he had not made love to Janet, though the offer had been there; that he was sexually frustrated as well as enraged; and that the control she always associated with him was at this moment barely on the edge—a very ragged edge. They stopped at a red light, long enough for Brian to turn the full force of those glinting black eyes on her. "Did he lay a finger on you, Leigh?" His jaw was clenched and his lips tight; he was a stranger she had never met before.

She took a breath. "Of course not," she said quietly. "Brian, how could you think that? I would never let anyone—"

"Wouldn't you?" he challenged. The light changed and his eyes left hers, but the tension in his tall, broad shoulders was unmistakable.

She remembered, suddenly, the way his eyes had trailed hers at dinner. She had thought he was trying to tell her what he wanted her to do in relation to the Rawlings, but she knew now that wasn't it. It was something between the two of them, and a fleeting instinct whispered that he was telling her that if anyone ever touched her it would be him, her husband. And was he also warning her that he *was* going to touch her, was going to rewrite the rules in that area as he had rewritten the rules of their social life? She felt a wild fluttering in the pit of her stomach and clenched her fists.

Silently, she huddled against the door of the car, feeling as unsafe and unsettled and thoroughly unhappy as she could remember, and said nothing at all to him for the entire ride home.

Two weeks before Christmas, a Saturday morning, Brian tracked her down in her study, where she had been working on a client's accounts. Now that the morning sickness had abated, she had begun working again, but as a freelance accountant and only part time. To return to White's and a full-time schedule would have been too demanding, and she had planned to work at home after the baby's birth anyway, as she would want to be around at least until the child was old enough for nursery school. It made sense to start accepting clients now.

"Sorry to interrupt," Brian apologized, "but I thought you'd want to see the letter we got from my mother this morning." He held out a sheet of yellow stationery.

Leigh took the missive and eagerly began to read it. Just after Brian had moved in with her, they had called his mother to tell her of the marriage. Despite her disappointment at having missed the ceremony, Mrs. Hathaway had been delighted with the news, and she and Leigh had immediately warmed to each other over the phone. At the older woman's suggestion, they had begun a correspondence, just the two of them, in addition to the letters Mrs. Hathaway often addressed to both Leigh and Brian. In that initial phone conversation, they had also arranged that Brian and Leigh would spend Christmas in Minnesota, so Leigh could meet her mother-in-law as well as Brian's brothers and their wives. The letter Leigh was reading now was full of happy anticipation over the upcoming visit.

"There's really no way we can get out of the trip," Brian commented, watching her intently. "As you can see, my mother's very excited about meeting you."

Leigh shot him a quizzical look. "I had no intention of trying to get out of the visit," she said calmly. "I've been looking forward to meeting your family, especially your mother; I already like her so much from her letters."

"I know," he said guardedly. "But you haven't forgotten what I told you about her?"

"I haven't forgotten," she murmured. He would have his mother believe they were a loving couple, which would mean a fair amount of physical contact between them. Affection. She glanced up at Brian, then away. Something was changing within her that she could not quite identify. More and more, she found herself eager for Brian's company, and at the same time the idea of touching him was beginning to haunt her, like an echo of something she couldn't have, would never have. "Since Robert's arranged to have one of his cronies spend the holidays here with him, and I'm feeling quite well enough to travel, I really see no problem about the trip," she said finally, looking directly into her husband's eyes.

His look was probing. "You have no problem with the idea of playing the loving couple?" he asked bluntly. "We're a demonstrative family, Leigh. My mother will expect us to be physically affectionate—more so than we've been in front of Robert or at the parties we've been going to lately."

"I understand that." Then she added softly, "I trust you, Brian."

For a moment, there was a stark, hollow look on his face that she'd never seen before, a tiny crack in the mosaic of her inscrutable husband. "I know," he said as he stood up. "I remember," he went on, "when I was a kid, one time I put together a model Jaguar. It took hours, all those tiny pieces, glue and wait, glue and wait. And when it was done, it was beautiful, Leigh, but very, very fragile. I took pride in having made it but there wasn't much joy in possessing something I couldn't play with or touch for fear of breaking it."

His tone was absent, almost as if he were thinking aloud instead of speaking to her. He paused momentarily in the doorway, and Leigh groped for something to say, not quite sure why he'd brought up the little anecdote. "Perhaps you should have played with it," she said lightly. "With all that glue and all . . ."

"That was a damned hard risk to take at eight years old."

She still didn't understand, but in a moment he was gone and she immersed herself in her accounts again, thinking with anticipation of the trip to Minnesota.

Chapter 9

IT WAS ONLY five o'clock in the morning when Brian opened the trunk of the car in the parking lot of Chicago's O'Hare airport. Blustery cold and still blue-black as night, there was nevertheless something about the crystal air that belonged to Christmastime.

Leigh's door was wrenched open as she knew it would be, and she looked unrepentantly at the grim set to Brian's features that she knew by now indicated a steel control on his emotions.

"Did I somehow neglect to mention to you that we're only going to be gone for two days?"

"I need every one of the suitcases," Leigh said calmly.

"You do *not* need five suitcases. We aren't taking them. And we've hardly got time to sort through the mess at this time of night!"

"They're presents, Brian," she explained.

"I *told* you . . ." He had told her to forgo buying presents, except for his mother. He didn't exchange gifts with his three brothers and their wives; they considered it a waste of time when it was so difficult to ascertain the needs, desires, and sizes of people living so many miles apart. Brian was shouting at Leigh, but only because the wind made normal voices inaudible, and she was shouting back. The presents were for the children. He had four nephews and two nieces, and one never forgot a child at Christmas, and there'd be no time for shopping once they got there. She was not going anywhere without the suitcases.

"So you hid them in the back, thinking I wouldn't find out until it was too late, did you?" He calmed visibly with an effort. "Leigh, we can send the presents later," he said patiently. "They won't let us take that much extra weight on board, can't you see that? At the very least, we're putting one suitcase in the trunk."

"All right." She motioned to the last, and then started out. Even though most of the cases were quite light, they were still bulky and cumbersome to carry. She had two, one of which slipped when Brian suddenly shouted out one more *"Leigh"* from behind her. She turned, feeling the icy wind on her cheeks.

"Just what was in the one you left behind?" he demanded ominously.

"My clothes," she said quietly.

"What?"

"MY CLOTHES!" she yelled, trying to make herself heard above the shriek of the wind.

He looked absolutely enraged with her for a minute, but it didn't last. It was becoming as fascinating as it was infuriating to watch him carefully don his figurative kid gloves, hiding his every emotion from her. He stomped back to the car, but did not say another word.

They were barely inside the crowded terminal before the loudspeaker announced that their flight would be delayed due to weather conditions. As Brian took care of the tickets and luggage, Leigh viewed the crowded terminal with mixed delight and dismay. People were everywhere, and there were no empty seats in sight. The enthusiasm of the holiday mood was catching, but it was also loud and boisterous.

"This way," Brian said abruptly, taking her arm as he led her past and through the milling crowd.

"Did you have trouble?" she asked guiltily, oddly conscious of the pressure of his fingers on her arm. His stride was impatient; Brian hated chaos. He flashed her a dark look, saying nothing. Obviously, he had handled it, and the children would have their presents. He led her down an all but empty corridor, pausing before a door into which he fitted a key. Inside was a small, windowless room, outfitted with a cot and huge, overstuffed chair, a coffeemaker, simple tables—and an instantly peaceful relief from the madding crowd.

"What is this?" Leigh asked curiously.

Brian removed his coat and settled in the chair with his briefcase. "Just put your feet up, Leigh. It's going to be a long day."

"You rented this room?" she persisted, still confused.

He shuffled through his papers, all but ignoring her. "At this time of year, an on-time takeoff would have been a miracle," he said absently. "So rather than standing for an indeterminate period of time . . ."

He left the rest unsaid. Thoughtfully, she removed her coat, revealing an apricot wool dress that clung to her rounded breasts, then flowed in loose swirls to her knees. She poured his coffee and then her own, studying him. A folder was perched on his bended knee. His absorption in his work was instant, but the black hair was still rumpled from their windy walk and his face still ruddy from the cold. He was preoccupied, with a moody air he did not normally wear. She backed up, without really knowing why, to a more shadowy corner, her coffee cup held in both hands as she leaned against the wall. Always in control, her Brian, especially where she was concerned. And suddenly she was uncomfortable with that—with his quick masking of his emotions whenever she was around, his treating her with kid gloves, his emotionless caretaking.

"Take off your shoes, Red, and lie down," he suggested idly, without looking up from his work.

"You got the room for me, didn't you?" she asked suddenly, warily.

"Hmmm?"

"Brian, what are you doing?" she whispered softly.

He looked up then. Lightning-fast, she felt his glance

take in the soft, alluring lines of her dress, the rich russet of her hair, the care she'd taken with her makeup. The results of the assessment she didn't know. She rarely knew. And that, too, was becoming irritating.

"I don't like it," she said stiffly. "I didn't expect this. A conventional wife would expect all kinds of consideration—but you married me because I don't, Brian, and you know that. So what are you *doing?*" There was a crazy desperate note in her voice that startled her.

Brian finally looked up, pinning her with a strangely intense black-eyed stare. "What am I doing?" he repeated lazily. "Taking care of you, my unconventional wife. In my own way."

The little silence was uncomfortable. Leigh looked down into her coffee cup and saw a distressed pair of topaz eyes reflected in the clear brown liquid. "I don't need taking care of. That's the point. This kind of thing—this room—isn't necessary."

"I'll decide what's necessary," he said tersely, returning to his work.

She set down her cup angrily. She didn't understand him, and because of that he frightened her, and even after all this time she couldn't rid herself of the feeling. Like a moth to the flame, she was increasingly drawn, increasingly repelled. Like a fool, she seemed to crave something from him, a closeness she had no right to want, more of the easiness they occasionally felt around each other. But what did *he* want? She was certain only that he wanted something different from her than what he'd originally told her.

It was not a long flight, hardly more than an hour. By the time they were in the air, Leigh's normal good humor had been restored. She was delighted to be going on this short vacation, had always loved the holidays, and it had been ages since she'd been part of an old-fashioned, big family celebration—exactly the kind Mrs. Hathaway had promised in her letters.

Leigh already knew a great deal about the family from her mother-in-law. Brian was the oldest of four boys; the other three were long married and had children. His father had died when Brian was a teenager, so his mother had depended on her first-born child to control the wild and rowdy group: highly competitive and argumentative, in and out of scrapes, boisterous . . . Secretly Leigh thought Mrs. Hathaway approved of all of it. In her letters, she came across as warmhearted, endowed with both intelligence and humor, and fiercely loyal to her sons. Richard was a doctor, Gerald owned a farm a distance from St. Paul, and Barry was an executive in business. In her letters, Mrs. Hathaway had made no secret of the fact that Brian was her favorite. When Mr. Hathaway died, she had worried that Brian was being forced to take on too much responsibility, and later she had despaired that he would ever be willing to settle down and take on a family of his own.

She'd also told Leigh that she already thought of her as a daughter, and hoped for a closeness between them that she already enjoyed with her other daughters-in-law: Jane, Julie, and Sandra. She had also hinted that she hoped Leigh would find in her a second mother rather than a mere in-law. "You haven't any parents, Leigh, and after four tries I gave up on having a daughter. As much as I love the boys, I've had men around me all my life, and frankly, at this point they're too much for me."

Leigh had thought the last comment rather strange, until she stepped off the plane with Brian behind her and saw three massive men with strong-featured faces dominating the busy airport crowd, striding toward her with a relentless determination against the surge of bodies. She nestled back against Brian, and then was all but wrenched from him, swept up from the ground and hugged and kissed by all three of his brothers. Brian was treated with an equally boisterous enthusiasm, and by the time he'd grabbed her hand and returned her to his side, she was laughing as hard as his brothers were.

The names and facts Mrs. Hathaway had imparted in her letters were immediately forgotten. They all looked so much alike, with their dark hair and black eyes, and they were, en masse, quite overpowering . . . and not. The laughter was spontaneous and nonstop, and Leigh felt a crazy high just from seeing them so rambunctious and just plain happy.

"I don't understand—did you pick this one with room to grow," Gerald teased. "Or are all the girls so tiny in Chicago, Brian?"

"Gerald was going to come alone," Barry volunteered, "but we decided we'd all better size her up at once. You don't mind, do you, Leigh?"

Three pair of midnight eyes surveyed her from head to toe, and three smiling faces beamed their approval. For once she did not care; their frank appreciation, instead of being disturbing, made her feel strangely lighthearted with laughter. She was a sister, just that quickly, a little old to be seeking the attention of big brothers, but that was part of it, too. She was surrounded by the four men as they made their way out of the terminal.

"The group's already at Mom's. We've got to get the tree yet this afternoon," Barry told Brian. "Christmas is at Gerald's tomorrow; he's the only one with a house big enough to hold all of us. Mother's orders are to feed Leigh and bring her right back, but—"

"We don't want to do that," Gerald interrupted. "You don't really want to be around a bunch of gossipy women, do you, Leigh? You'll have time for all that later. We'll still have you home in a couple of hours. Otherwise, it's a separate trip back there and—"

"Leigh's not only been up since five," Brian interjected swiftly, "but she's hardly dressed for an outing."

"That doesn't matter," she intervened just as swiftly, not wanting to upset any plans.

"I really think—"

"Brian!" As the other three forged ahead through the snow with the suitcases, Leigh murmured to Brian, "They can't go all the way back to your mother's just to let me off. I'm perfectly all right." His hand on her shoulder tightened possessively and she glanced up, startled to see the warm amusement in his dark eyes.

"'All the way back to Mother's,'" he repeated teasingly. "Just how far do you think that is—Siberia? You don't have the least idea what you're letting yourself in for, Red."

His three brothers had stopped at a newish green station wagon, and the luggage was being stowed in back. "Besides, I know you want to go with them," she pointed out, watching

Barry and Gerald climb into the front and Richard get in the back. She glanced up again to see Brian's jaw set at a stubborn angle. "I'm perfectly capable of deciding whether or not I'm tired," she argued.

"Come *on,* you two!"

Determinedly, she bent to get in the backseat next to Richard, and felt an admonishing thump on her backside. Her jaw all but dropped at the unexpected familiarity, and then Brian was wedged in beside her. There was suddenly no room to breathe as she sat between the broad shoulders of Richard and Brian; the car was not the largest of station-wagon models.

"So what's it to be, boss?" Gerald asked Brian as he started the engine.

Brian suddenly grasped her by the waist and shifted her onto his lap so that she was sitting sideways with her back to the door, facing Richard who took the immediate opportunity to stretch out his legs. "More comfortable, Leigh?" Brian asked blandly, and to the others, "The redhead insists she's going—as long as we've got some way of keeping her warm."

She only half heard the rest of the conversation, though the men's chatter was continuous throughout the drive. She caught certain inferences: that in some way she had surprised the brothers; that Brian was consulted on every turn as if old habits were reasserting themselves; that she and Brian were under intense and awed scrutiny, as if the brothers had never expected to catch Brian acting possessive or affectionate—or like a newlywed.

But Leigh knew it was all just an illusion, an illusion Brian had created by seating her easily on his lap, pretending there was no awkwardness to her stiff form, forcing a closeness he had never forced before. His coat was open and her coat and dress had been mortifyingly rearranged in the shift; the top of his thighs were warm and hard and intimate underneath her own. His arms were clasped loosely around her waist. When the car heated up, he raised a hand to unbutton the two top buttons of her coat as he talked, his fingers lingering on the erratic pulse at her throat, then up, brushing an errant strand of dark copper hair first from one cheek, then the other. His fingertips lingered on the soft skin of her face and then trailed down to her throat, threading in her hair just beneath her ear to encourage her cheek to the rough texture of his coat. "Relax, Leigh," he murmured, his lips a sensual whisper in her ear.

Leigh could not move. She had been prepared to play the game of closeness for the sake of his family—a kiss in front of the Christmas tree, a hand on her shoulder, a warm hug in front of his mother, perhaps a casual caress or two. But this did not feel like a game. It felt like a very private world where only the two of them knew certain secrets, where the two of them were making secrets, and the intimacy Brian was establishing was in deadly earnest. His strength increasingly held mixed messages for her—a protective promise and yet a threat more potent than the one she had lived with in her nightmares. She wished suddenly that she had never met him, even as she found herself beginning to relax and feel comfortably cozy on his lap.

"Here we are! Come on, Leigh, we're going to set you up so warm you'll think you're in the tropics. Unhand her, Brian, for heaven's sake. Does he let you go to the mailbox all by yourself?" Barry asked Leigh teasingly.

They got out of the car, and the air was crisp and bright, brilliantly clear. Two feet of snow covered the forested area, and outside an old two-story barn a horse-drawn sleigh from a bygone era looked ready to be used. They were at Gerald's farm, and less than fifteen minutes later they were skimming over the snow according to an old family tradition. Leigh had a thick fur pelt over her lap, and Brian's arm was around her to keep off the stinging wind that whipped up color in her cheeks. She was freezing, lightheaded with the rushing sensation of sheer exhilaration. When the men stopped the sleigh, the fur rugs were wrapped tightly around her before they traipsed off with ax in tow to argue over the choice of a Christmas tree in the middle of the Minnesota woods— and they *did* argue. She had a vision of exactly how it must have been when they were boys. The pines were blanketed with white; there was no possible way to judge shape or size, and still they argued. As they shook the snow from the trees to make more accurate assessments, the arguments culminated in a playful snowball fight—but at last Brian broke up the nonsense, the ax was put to work, and then the sleigh was skimming the open fields again.

"So what do you think, Leigh?" Richard called out from the front seat.

She laughed with sheer delight, loving all of it—Christmas, the tree, the lovely sleigh, the brothers, the clearest day she had ever seen. "I didn't know families really did this! I love it!"

Barry nodded next to her. "I guess we'll keep you, Shorty. You cold, darlin'?"

She was freezing. "Of course not! I'm fine!"

"I believe I already mentioned that if she got cold I was going to kill all of you," Brian mentioned pleasantly, and the other three hooted at him.

"Listen to him!" Richard howled. "He's got it so bad he's nearly a basket case. Oh, have *you* come down like a mortal!"

"All these years we've envied your bachelor status. How are the mighty fallen!"

It was so very different from what they thought! The pretense had worked like a charm with Brian's brothers, yet Leigh wondered fleetingly if his mother would be so easy to fool.

Chapter 10

RUTH HATHAWAY WAS as gregarious, warm, and lively as her letters had indicated, but much more petite than Leigh had pictured her. Indeed, she was startled to see the little bit of white-haired fluff who came storming out to the car without a coat. No one that tiny could conceivably have given birth to the four tall Hathaway men!

"I told you to bring her right home! Now she'll be too tired to talk. You boys are so thoroughly selfish at times that I'm tempted to take a hairbrush to the lot of you! Oh, Brian! Aren't you as handsome as ever!" She hugged and kissed her son and then Leigh, accepted all the apologies that were due her, and with one arm about Leigh and one about Brian, she led them into the house.

"Leigh, you're beautiful! And not painted-mannequin beautiful, but the genuine article. Brian, you've got a lot more sense than I ever gave you credit for, or should I be giving you all the credit, Leigh? Come in, I'll get you something to drink; you'll have to meet everyone. We've got hamburgers grilling on the fire for dinner and we're eating in shifts—there's just no room to do it any other way—and then we'll put up the tree. If you're just so tired you can't stand up, you could rest for a bit, Leigh—"

"She is," Brian interrupted.

"I'm not," Leigh lied.

It was more a cottage than a house, small enough for Mrs. Hathaway's needs but very obviously not the place where she had raised her four sons. The room they entered was a fairly large one, but so crowded that it seemed quite small. Children were everywhere, and the three sisters-in-law sat on antique furniture clustered around a massive stone fireplace. Pictures, pillows, and hand-knit afghans added color and clutter. Leigh's suitcases were taken to a room off the left, and from the right she saw the hallway to the kitchen, but other than this, she could guess nothing about the rest of the house.

Suddenly, a bundle of dark curls launched herself at Leigh. "You're Aunt Leigh? Do you know who's coming tonight?" Leigh was almost pushed into a chair so that the cherubic-looking little girl could sit in her lap.

"Santa?" Leigh guessed.

"I'm Julia," said one of the women with long, plaited dark hair and a bright ski outfit. "This is Jane"—she pointed to a rather homely woman in jeans and a man's flannel shirt who had a wonderfully welcoming smile—"and this is Sandra." Sandra was much more chic than the other two, in a cranberry jumpsuit that accented her blond coloring.

"You're wearing my favorite color," the cherub announced from Leigh's lap. The women laughed, and tried to identify for Leigh which of the offspring playing around the room belonged to whom. The men were bringing in the tree, and Mrs. Hathaway never stopped talking.

"My name is Ruth, Leigh, but I'd much rather you called me Mother. Julia, Jane, and Sandra do."

"I'm Brandy," the dark-eyed cherub offered.

"How *could* you get another lopsided tree? A whole forest to choose from . . ."

"No shaking those presents, young man, or Santa may just cross you right off his list!"

"Do you want a little wine, Leigh?"

She was suddenly overwhelmed—oh, but in a thoroughly wonderful way. She would have loved to play with the bright-eyed children, or chat with her mother-in-law, or answer her sisters-in-law's questions, or even help trim the tree, but it couldn't be done, not at once. It had been too long since she'd had something in her stomach, and they had already been up for twelve hours, and the contrast between the freezing, brisk air and this cozy but stiflingly warm room . . .

The child was lifted off her lap, and Brian swept Leigh up in his arms and carted her off to the room where the suitcases had been put. Without any ceremony, he pushed the door shut with his foot, set her on the double bed, and briskly unzipped the back of her dress as he pressed her head down between her knees.

"I've never fainted in my life!" she wailed dizzily.

"You don't regularly turn green either, Red. Are you sick to your stomach as well?"

She resented the question, refusing to answer it. "I'm going right back," she mumbled.

"Sure you are. Why don't you move one inch off the bed and see what happens to you?" Brian suggested mildly. From behind her, his cool hands splayed firmly around her collarbones. His palm heated to the warmth of her skin, and slowly he massaged the tension away, soothing in an almost ridiculous sensation of well-being and peace. Long after the overheated sense of dizziness had passed, she stayed still, inhaling the sensual comfort he offered, the peace, the privacy of just the two of them.

"Honey, are you ill?" The door opened as Brian's mother stepped inside. Ruth spoke more slowly than before, with genuine concern.

"I don't know what happened—I'm so sorry, Mrs. Hathaway. Really, I'm perfectly fine." Brian's fingers refused to release her, tightening just perceptibly when she tried to get up. Thoughts jumbled in her mind like jigsaw-puzzle pieces as Brian brushed aside her hair and zipped up her dress. A possessive and thoroughly experienced gesture, she thought irrelevantly. And that was just it. How easy it was for him to play the possessive and protective and loving husband. Suddenly Leigh felt a pang that it was all nothing but pretense, for that afternoon *she* had not entirely been pretending. In the midst of this warm, loving family, she had felt the icy chill that had so long surrounded her heart begin to thaw.

"She's pregnant, Mom," Brian said quietly.

"A baby! But neither of you said a word! Oh, my dears!" A kiss was extended to both of them, and a double hug for Leigh. But then Ruth Hathaway cast a cold, stern look at her son. "Because it's Christmas, I won't even scold you for carting this pregnant child all over the countryside." She paused deliberately, and Leigh began to see just how she had managed to raise four rowdy boys, and to realize that her mother-in-law was no bit of fluff, for all her chatter. "We'll get you something to eat and a place to put your feet up, Leigh, and it'll be an early night for you. Just get out of here, Brian, and fix up a plate for her."

When Brian was gone, his mother fluffed up the pillows and drew down the spread, encouraging Leigh to rest a little longer. "It'll give us a few more minutes of peace before we face the confusion again," she said sympathetically. "Brian always said that's what drove him nuts about the family: no peace, no privacy, and continual confusion. You're two of a kind, aren't you?"

"Oh, but I love families, Mrs. Hathaway," Leigh protested.

"Mother," she corrected gently. "And of course you do. But one can raise families in chaos—heaven knows that was my style—or with serenity, the way I'm sure you will."

Leigh ate with a tray on her lap and Brian at her side. The tree was trimmed, mostly by the children, with handmade decorations they had brought with them, and with long strings of popcorn that had gaping holes where the goodies had inevitably been filched. There were a few tears over candy canes that weren't to be eaten yet, and arguments and laughter over the placement of the tinsel, and then it was done. The tree lights were put on, the fire roared in the fireplace, and all the other lights were turned off.

A hushed silence fell on the group. It was one of the most magical moments Leigh could remember. The tired yawns and smiles of the children, so wide-eyed in anticipation, so quiet now . . . the brothers instinctively paired off

with their wives, inevitably close in the crowded room...
Mrs. Hathaway beaming at all of them from her Bentwood
rocker... and Brian, one arm nestled around Leigh's rib
cage, the smell of his clean hair, and the touch of the bristles
on his chin as she leaned back in his shoulder, cuddling
against his neck. Her palm slid up to his chest and rested
there. For just that moment there were no fears and no past
and nothing intruding on her consciousness. A yearning
surged through her, alien and surprising, a yearning to stay
this close to Brian and... even more.

People tiptoed past, one family after another, the young-
est of the children carried sleepily by their parents. Still,
for a long time afterward Mrs. Hathaway continued to rock
contentedly in front of the tree, and Brian did not disturb
the tresses on his shoulders that gleamed red-gold in the
firelight.

In the way of dreams, myriad sensations touched her
consciousness and passed by, replaced by others. She was
drifting through clouds in slow motion, her skin brush-
painted with the softness of fleeting white puffs of air. Then
she was running through a meadow of spring flowers, on a
hot summer's day, her bare feet meeting the sponge of thick
grasses, with a sensation of running *to* rather than away
from... Another sensation, the best: floating in water at
midnight, the sea swaddling her like liquid silk, caressing
and enclosing her in warm moistness. She had never felt so
safe, so warm, so cloaked in the most luxurious textures;
even her breasts felt cupped in a protective velvet shield... not
velvet...

Her eyes opened to full and instant wakefulness. Her
naked back was to Brian's chest; his arms around her and
his hands cradling both of her breasts. She could feel the
warmth of his fingers enclosing her taut nipples. Beneath a
mountain of quilts, he didn't seem to be wearing anything
either. Shock stilled her breathing; and then, convinced from
the total silence behind her that he was asleep, she tried to
inch away, to get out of the bed and away from him. His
fingers suddenly gripped her breasts more tightly, and she
whirled to find his eyes boring into hers, as wide awake as
her own.

"Good Lord, what are you doing here?" she hissed. "What are you doing?"

The room was freezing when she pushed back the covers, and for a confused instant she simply lay back again, settling for heaping the covers as a barrier between them. Brian continued to stare at her from beneath his rumpled matt of dark hair.

"This is the only bedroom," he answered quietly. "It's a two-room bungalow, plus the kitchen."

"And you knew that—before? Of course, I assumed we'd have to sleep in the same room, but I didn't realize there'd be only the one bed—not even a couch or an armchair or—" Panic and fury knotted in her throat, half-choking her. Of course *he* knew that. "You can't sleep here, Brian!"

"I just did," he pointed out dryly. "And very well. You're a kitten when you sleep, Red, all curled up."

She turned her head away, taking a strangled breath. "We can't stay here tonight, not like this. You'll have to do something."

"Red," he said, "there is no alternative, and we *are* going to sleep here again tonight in the same bed. And yes, I expect you are a little ticked off; but then, it proved a number of things, didn't it?"

"What?" she snapped.

"To you, I wanted to prove I wasn't going to rape you— for once and for all. And if you turn those frightened eyes on me just one more time, I'm liable to take you over my knee or shake it out of you—one or the other. Do you hear me?"

He sounded angry, but she was the one with cause for anger. She had been tricked into coming here for the holidays, when he knew what the sleeping arrangements would be. But her initial fury faded. The panicky, sick sensation of dread was more powerful; it always had been.

"But I was trying to prove something to me, too, Leigh," Brian went on. "Something I've suspected for a while. You led me to believe you were dead inside sexually, that there was some man you were holding a torch for so you didn't want any other kind of involvement with anyone. And how well I thought that suited us, two cynical people who knew better than to get too involved."

"I *am* dead inside," she said tightly. "I don't know what you're trying to—"

"Either you're lying to me or you're lying to yourself." Abruptly his tone softened, and he turned to look at her. When she averted her face from his too perceptive eyes, his arm reached out from under the warmth of the quilt to force her gaze to meet his. "Leigh, you're not only not dead, you're so much alive it hurts. It's hurting you all the time. You slide away from every touch like quicksilver. But there've been times, Red, when you haven't had the time to think, when you've all but asked for someone to hold on to—"

"Never," she denied, trying to twist her face away. He snatched at her hands and held them still between his.

"You're afraid." His steel voice was low and gravelly. "It isn't that you don't feel. It isn't that there's someone else. It isn't that you don't want—"

"Don't!" she hissed desperately, closing her eyes so she wouldn't have to look at him. "What I *feel* has nothing to do with anything! Brian, we were doing fine; we could still be doing fine. Don't pry, or you'll ruin everything!"

She turned over so that her back was to him. She would have leapt from the bed if his hands hadn't suddenly closed like a vise on both sides of her waist from behind. She froze, facing a white-curtained window, not moving for fear of inviting more contact. It was enough, his palms on her hips and his fingers laced across the smooth, warm flesh of her stomach. He didn't hurt her, but there was enough tension in his hold to convince her she wasn't getting up, not that easily.

"And then I thought something else, Red," he said softly. "That your aversion was simply for me. A physical antipathy of some kind—and that was quite a blow to my ego. But then I saw that it applies to other men even more than to me, so—"

"I don't want to discuss it!"

She started trembling. Helplessly, she felt the arm encircling her waist draw her back to the cradle of his chest,

and felt his lips touching the nape of her neck, teasing, soothingly soft. "Convince me, Red," he said in a low voice.
"Convince me you feel nothing at all for me, and I'll never
so much as touch you again."

"Don't," she pleaded softly. "Please don't."

His hard thigh drew against the back of her leg and she
felt a shudder pass through her. The trembling had intensified. He leaned just over the back of her, slowly smoothing
the protective blanket of her hair from her face. His expression as he bent down was intense, even grave, his lips
smooth and warm, closing her eyes, following the trail of
his fingers. "I think you're shaking because you *do* want
me, and it frightens you. I won't settle for that, Leigh. I
won't allow fear—not with me."

His hand crept up from her waist and cupped a breast.
The creamy globe was tender; her breasts had been sensitive
for some time now, swelling with the knowledge of the
child within her, but under his palms the nipples became as
hard as pebbles. Her skin felt strangely warm wherever he
touched; his touch was as firm as it was gentle, and so
loving that she felt oddly, frighteningly weak.

"I have no intention of making love to you, Leigh," he
whispered. "Not here, not now. I like complete privacy for
real lovemaking."

She breathed a little, closing her eyes. He murmured
something approving when a little of the tension left her,
and cradled her closer yet to his chest. He was so warm,
and his palms stroked more warmth down the still curve of
her hip and up to the small contour of her stomach. His
palm rested for a moment between her breasts, willing her
heartbeat to still its pounding, then moved up to the sensitive
hollow of her throat. The sensations were terrible: the fear
threatening to make her physically ill; and a wanting, newly
born, fragile but far stronger than she could understand. She
ached, suddenly and desperately, inside. It struck her that
there was still a chance—that if she turned to him Brian
might . . . be able to make her forget about David, and she
could almost imagine losing herself in that gentle, sensual
world of his touch. But there was a greater chance that she
couldn't, that she would merely open a Pandora's box and
find herself incapable of responding, numb, frozen, as she

had been with Peter. And she suddenly understood how very little Peter had ever meant to her in comparison. Not for Brian, an ice maiden; never could she risk that.

The rap on the door was startling, like a shower turned cold.

"Leigh? Brian?" Mrs. Hathaway rapped again and then opened the door. "I thought I heard the sound of voices. Merry Christmas, you two. It's time you were up. I've got breakfast on the stove."

She closed the door again and Leigh turned over to stare into Brian's dark eyes, which were dilated still, midnight black. "Merry Christmas," he echoed, and dipped his head for a very quick and passionless kiss on her nose. "Your heart's going at the same rate mine is," he whispered teasingly. "Tell me about indifference, Red. Tell me how you feel nothing."

"Brian—"

He bounded out of bed to the bathroom. "Sorry, Leigh, but the subject's been tabled, not closed."

He left the bathroom door more than half open as he took a quick shower, with a thorough lack of modesty that appalled Leigh. It was as if, on the sheer arrogance of a whim, Brian had decided to change everything and so he was doing it all at once. She leapt from the bed, deciding to forgo bathroom privileges until later, and quickly put on underwear and then a winter-white angora skirt and sweater that were as soft as they were festive. Not too formal for a day that would include playing with children.

Brian had finished his shower and was standing in the doorway to watch as she straightened the bed. There was only a towel slung carelessly around his waist, and his face had a full white beard of shaving cream. The hairs on his chest still glistened from the water in the shower, and the smooth slope of his shoulders was a reminder of the physical strength inherent in his long, lean body. She hurried to bring the covers into some kind of order.

"You know," he said conversationally, "for someone so indifferent to 'matters of the flesh,' Red, you shocked the hell out of me when I undressed you last night. You really think that little bit of powder-blue lace has any support to it?"

"Stop it," she hissed, a dark flush staining her cheeks. She couldn't find her shoes; there were so many suitcases and such a jumbled disorder of wrapped packages for the children. And she had to find the present for his mother.

"I was even a little worried—you've got such a tiny little curve of a stomach that it was almost impossible to believe you were pregnant. The whole package is still bikini material, Red, and when I think of how you had me totally fooled when I first met you—"

She didn't have the nerve to slam the door on the way out, for fear Mrs. Hathaway would hear the sound.

Chapter 11

LEIGH FELT AS though she had finally stepped off a roller coaster when the door was closed behind her. It was all so simple, really. It was Christmas and nothing should be allowed to happen that would mar the holiday, if only because there were other peole involved. And Brian . . . Perhaps it was just an insane moment. Perhaps if she just ignored what had happened—or maybe she could talk to Mrs. Hathaway. There must be some other place to sleep. A couch—she could say that she was sleeping poorly because of the pregnancy, that Brian's tossing and turning disturbed her.

But Leigh did nothing of the kind. Mrs. Hathaway teased her over the breakfast table about how absolutely soundly she had slept curled next to Brian the evening before, and not even the comings and goings of twelve people had stirred her. Brian's mother looked absolutely stunning in a cherry-red dress that set off her white hair; she looked like Christmas itself, with a sprig of holly pinned on her collar. "I'm sorry for all the confusion yesterday, Leigh. I wanted so much to have some time with you, just ourselves, to get to know one another, but it's impossible with the holidays. I know Brian said he had to leave tomorrow, but couldn't *you* just stay a little longer?"

Brian arrived just then to help himself to enough bacon and eggs and fried potatoes to bring a smile of satisfaction from his mother. "She can't, Mom," he said definitely. "For one thing, I don't want her flying back alone in her condition. And the airports are a mess this time of year; I don't want her stuck standing around for hours at a stretch."

"Well, then," Mrs. Hathaway answered, her brown eyes darting back and forth between the two of them, "what I'd like, Leigh, if it's all right with you, is to come when you have the baby and you need some help."

"I'd love that," Leigh answered warmly. Nevertheless, she thought uneasily of having to share a room with Brian for the duration of his mother's visit. At least she could make sure they had separate beds.

After church they drove to Gerald's in the station wagon, the backseat laden with packages. The doors to the big frame farmhouse opened at their arrival, and a host of welcoming children and adults poured out. A horde of dogs seemed to descend on Leigh as she got out of the car, barely letting her pass as they crowded around her legs. Her arms were as full of presents as Brian's and his mother's.

The presents were pounced on first, because the children simply couldn't wait, regardless of all the mothers clucking behind them. Mrs. Hathaway chuckled as the area under the tree became cluttered with piles of wrapping paper, boxes, and ribbons. "I like a big spread under the tree," she admitted frankly. "I used to individually wrap practically every crayon, just so they'd all have dozens of things to open!"

The mothers scolded Leigh for going to so much trouble over the children's presents, but the children were delighted with these unexpected packages to open—and delighted with their new aunt, who didn't hesitate to sit in the middle of the mess with them, who didn't mind if her soft angora sweater was fingered even if the fingers were slightly sticky. She was not opposed to ribbons being stuck in her hair, and she knew enough to throw a bit of zinc from Barry Junior's

new chemistry set on the fire to magically turn the flames
green and blue.

Finally, after the children's packages were opened, ex-
amined, discussed, and played with, Brian distributed the
adult's presents. Leigh had exchanged hugs and kisses with
Brian's three brothers and sisters-in-law, had responded to
and handed back compliments on dress, and had been teased
about the ease with which she was fitting in with the children. Yet through it all her awareness was intensely focused
on Brian, as if he were the only one in the room.

She had already seen him forbiddingly distant, occasionally humorous, elegant and charming when it suited
him, many times impatient, exasperatingly arrogant and
domineering—and he was a blend of all of that with his
family—but now she was beginning to see that even with
them he could not be completely himself. In two short hours,
Leigh had heard snatches of conversation directed at Brian:
Richard, explaining why he didn't want an expensive medical practice and the troubles he was having with Julie about
it; Barry, seeking approval for a job change he had made;
Gerald, with money troubles on the farm and an expansion
he wasn't sure of; and even Jane asked if one o'clock would
suit Brian for the family dinner.

She felt proud that his family so obviously respected and
needed him. But she could also see, too clearly, what was
behind his resistance to the image of home, family, and
clinging ties. She could even see why he might have sold
his soul for a marriage of convenience. His business was
draining enough; his bachelor social life had put another
series of demands on him; and his mother and brothers made
others. To look at him, one would never know he minded,
but Leigh could sense his resentment. He gave and gave
and gave; why couldn't anyone just ask him how *he* was,
whether he had any problems he needed to talk over?

Ruth settled in the chair behind Leigh and bent over to
whisper in her ear. "Stop staring, darling. Though he is the
handsomest of the four, isn't he?"

Embarrassed to be caught staring at her own husband,
Leigh gave her mother-in-law a bashful smile.

"I worried about him a long time," Ruth continued in a
half-whisper. "He isn't an easy man to love, because he

fights it so. It's always been easy for him to take responsibility, but he has trouble dealing with the softer emotions. He had it hard, when his father died, and it was up to him."

Leigh glanced at her mother-in-law and then away. It was true that he resisted any attention coming his way. It was all right for Brian to dose out consideration when it suited him, but all Leigh had to do was reveal the slightest bit of concern for his welfare and he clammed up, granite-faced. She had assumed he simply didn't feel the "softer" emotions; they were two of a kind, he had said.

"Come on, Red, open up." Presents replaced the wriggling child in her lap, and Brian slid down next to her, his long legs struggling to find space between the jumble of toys strewn everywhere. Even inches apart, she could feel the electricity between them, an unwilling current that refused to shut itself off. She was beginning to feel as vulnerable as dew whenever he was close—hopeless, helpless, and strangely intoxicated. She blinked back the sensations.

"You open first," she insisted. She had found it almost impossible to come up with an appropriate gift for Brian. He had everything practical, and anything sentimental might have been awkward. The dress watch she'd finally selected told time with two diamonds for hands, and was as masculine as it was unusual. She looked anxiously for his approval.

"How beautiful, Leigh," he said softly, and set it on his wrist to admire it. Lazily, his eyes flicked over her as well, as if the compliment applied even more to her. "Come on, open up! There's one here, and I'll bring the other in a minute."

She opened the small, flat package carefully. Inside was a necklace with a large black opal on a delicate chain. It was simple in design, yet stunning. She looked at him, not bothering to hide the glow in her eyes. "I love it, Brian. I didn't expect..." She reached up to kiss him swiftly. Very swiftly. Yet long enough to taste the soft, warm pressure and flavor of his mouth, which gave beneath hers. She drew back, and just as softly, just as swiftly, his finger traced the curl of her bottom lip. The flair of desire in his eyes startled her, but instantly it was gone. "I have to go out to get your other present, Red. Don't move."

The others were watching her now, their presents already opened. There was a special interest in what Brian said and did, and then there was the special interest that any newly-weds evoked. Moments later, Brian returned and stopped at the doorway. "I couldn't wrap this one. Will it offend your dignity if I ask you to close your eyes for five seconds, Red?" he asked teasingly.

Laughing and a little embarrassed, she agreed. It was only moments later that she felt a squirming weight on her lap and the sensation of wet silk lapping her palm. She opened her eyes, startled. A soft, curly-haired black puppy wriggled on the white angora of her skirt, its huge eyes staring into hers.

Slowly, gently, she bent to cuddle the animal, lifting it to the curve of her neck, her eyes lowered to blink back the glisten of tears. A gift of life was a gift of love, and she was suddenly conscious that it was Brian who had offered her both in the child growing within her. Overwhelmed, she could only stare mutely at the soft bundle of fur on her lap.

"Now, I know a pup's trouble, Red," Brian said, strangely tentative in her continued silence. "But he's one of Gerry's Newfoundlands—he'll grow into a good-sized watchdog, and the breed loves kids. I know I never asked if you liked animals, but I'd feel easier on the nights I work late . . ."

He stopped talking when she looked up at him. The amber of flame met charcoal, ignited, took hold. He was still standing, and between holding the pup and her skirts it was awkward to rise gracefully, and her shoes were gone. None of it was easy, to share from the heart she'd sheltered so fiercely. But it was necessary—that kind of honesty, that kind of acknowledgment for what his gifts had meant to her. Her fingers clenched in the fabric of his shirt as she reached up on tiptoe, her eyes never leaving his. Slowly, her lashes shuttered down as her mouth blended with his, her arms slipping around his waist to hold him.

His mouth deepened on hers, arching her throat back. It was Brian who pulled back, his eyes telling her he had only done so because of their audience, his face softer than she had ever seen it, as he kept his arms loosely around her.

"I think she likes the puppy better than the necklace," Barry teased lightly.

"Hey, Leigh, I've got a horse I'd be willing to give you right now, if you want to take a little trip out to the barn," Gerald suggested with a playful wink.

"Boys!" Mrs. Hathaway admonished, and they all started laughing, the children clamoring at Leigh's side, proud that they had kept the secret, demanding to play with the puppy.

The mood was broken as Jane called for help in the kitchen. The rest of the day sped by in a blur of activity: a large turkey dinner and a sleigh ride afterward; then a snowmobile ride and a snowball fight with children and adults alike. It was dark before Brian insisted they get ready to go back to his mother's house; there was a plane to Chicago to catch in the morning. Confusion accelerated promptly: presents were gathered, good-byes and thank you's expressed yet again. An impromptu round of turkey sandwiches was made and munched on, and an occasional child cried over broken toys or shrieked in play. Mrs. Hathaway obviously loved every minute of it, and added to the chaos by trying to finish any number of conversations she had previously started, all at the same time.

Leigh could not remember a day when she had laughed so much. She named the pup Monster as it climbed back and forth between the three of them, claiming constant attention the entire ride home. Brian took care of settling him when they reached Mrs. Hathaway's. Weariness overtook Leigh as she walked in the door, but it was a marvelously pleasant sensation. Mrs. Hathaway urged her into a warm tub, liberally sprinkled with scented bath salts. It was only nine-thirty when she emerged, clean and thoroughly at peace, sweet-smelling and snug in a soft velvet robe. Going to the living room she curled up on the couch by the Christmas tree, where Mrs. Hathaway was already settled in her rocker, knitting. "Brian's taken a short walk to wind down," she explained.

Leigh hugged her knees to her chest, staring mesmerized at the lights of the tree. Mrs. Hathaway seemed to be no more inclined to talk than she was. It had been a good day, and in spite of herself Leigh fought sleep, wanting to savor the memories.

She did not realize until Brian walked back in, stomping the snow from his boots, his features reddened with cold,

that somewhere inside she'd been waiting for his return so
that she could relax completely. Which made no sense—it
even struck a chord of disquiet inside. Yet before he had
finished the first shot of whiskey he poured to warm himself,
her head had fallen against the pillow and she was fast
asleep.

Leigh was seventeen in the dream. It was one in the
morning and she'd been out with Bob, one of her more
steady dates, celebrating his birthday present—a fancy, low-
slung sports car. Leigh neither liked nor disliked Bob, but
he suited—for the time being: his parents didn't care what
time she came in at night, and Leigh had her own reasons
for staying out late.

When she came home, she found her stepfather waiting
for her at the door. David's shirt was only half-buttoned,
and she could see that he'd been drinking. She was wary
of him, as she had been wary of him for months now; that
was the reason why she never came home nights until she
had to. This night was worse, because her mother was in
New York on a shopping trip and had left Leigh alone with
David, except for Robert on the opposite side of the house.

He insisted she have a drink with him, and rather than
cause a scene she agreed. The cards were still on the table
in the study; his poker-playing friends couldn't have been
gone long. The room was smoky; and there was an empty
liquor bottle on the table and another open at the bar. He'd
lost at cards; she knew that. It bothered him to lose, but
not to spend her mother's money doing it, a fact Leigh was
foolish enough to point out to him.

That was always the end of the floating sensation of the
dream and the beginning of the nightmare. She cringed in
sleep, seeing herself all too clearly in the dim smoky room,
so foolishly, innocently arrogant, proud of her contempt.
"Next to my father, you're such a parasite . . . what my mother
ever saw in you . . ." She was wrong to talk that way, but
he should never have brought up her mother, should never
have told Leigh that the only thing he'd ever seen in Andrea
Sexton was money . . . and her daughter. "I've just been
biding my time, waiting to be alone with you, sweetie," he
told her in a voice thick with whiskey.

The world crashed—confusion and darkness and shock. Her blouse was ripped and she was frantically trying to get to her feet, to get away from him. A slap on the side of her head sent her reeling. Before she'd recovered he was on top of her. She was sobbing with nausea and horror and disgust. "Oh no, oh no!"

He was stronger than she was, and drunk and insane, yet she kept believing he would stop, that he would never do this to her. But there had come a point when she knew she no longer had a chance of escaping from him, and the fear and horror were so great that her mind simply went blank. Responding to her instinct for survival, she lay still and closed her eyes, willing herself not to be sick, afraid he might kill her if she was. Her sudden lack of struggle saved her. The hands mauled her, intimately hurting, deliberately and viciously intent on rape. But he could not. She was not experienced enough in the ways of men to understand that her struggles had excited him, and her passivity unmanned him. She only knew that as long as she lay there and did absolutely nothing, he would not complete the final act of degradation.

Her stepfather raged, screamed, blaming her for his own failure. She opened her eyes, unable to hide the contempt and hatred she felt for him. He slapped one cheek and then the other, back and forth, back and forth. Instinct told her to remain still; even as her mind screamed with pain—a long, endless scream that no one ever heard.

"Oh, my God! No more! I can't take any more!"

"Leigh!"

Relief at having been startled from the nightmare was accompanied by huge shudders wracking her body. There were no tears. There hadn't been any tears in a long time.

Brian's hand reached for her shoulders to pull her closer, and she jerked away. "Oh God, don't touch me!" In a moment, she could feel his weight lifted from the bed and she was alone. She realized then that Brian must have carried her from the couch to the bedroom, but she didn't dwell on the thought. She huddled into a ball, trying to feel warm again, waiting for the shaking to stop. She took deep breaths of air, her heart thudding so fast it was an active pain in her chest.

It startled her anew when he returned and switched on the bedside lamp.

"Please," she whispered.

He switched it off again and crossed the room to raise the window shades instead. The glistening reflection of moonlight on snow turned the room from black to light charcoal. He approached the bed; lifting her up to a sitting position with no-nonsense firmness, then folding both her hands around a warm mug. "Drink it," he ordered. "Now, Leigh."

The hot milk was calming, soothing, and she drank it all. He took the mug from her hands and she covered her face with trembling fingers. She felt the weight of his body on the other side of the bed, and with her hands still over her eyes she was shifted into the cradle of his shoulder, her legs remaining tucked up to her chest. She was a mindless ball of shuddering; but gradually the warmth of his body infused a feeling of life into her, and the shuddering passed.

"That's the nightmare, is it?" he asked quietly. "The one Robert referred to. At the time, I conjectured it had to do with the death of a lover, but it's something else—worse—isn't it?"

She nodded. The shadows of it still encroached on her consciousness.

"Tell me, Leigh," he said gently.

She couldn't. It was bad enough to relive the trauma in nightmares without having to think it through in reality. And she couldn't tell Brian. Not Brian. Her voice was husky and bitter. "Telling isn't going to make it go away."

But he wasn't going to let her go until she obeyed. He'd already gotten a hint from her frantic whimperings when she was still asleep. Even to her own ears, Leigh's voice sounded ragged as she told him the story as if it had happened to someone else; it *had* happened to someone else. She was no longer that innocent girl on that long-ago night, and she never could be again.

When she'd finally gotten away from her stepfather, she had pulled together a blanket and robe and hidden in Robert's apartment, because she couldn't think of anything else to do. She hadn't awakened him, just slept on the floor by the old man's bed. But when he woke in the morning and saw her...."He tried to get me to go to a doctor, but I wouldn't. What was the point?" she said to Brian. "They were just bruises, a few cuts."

The words tumbled out, in almost incoherent whispers, an avalanche she could not stop. "The worst of it was that nothing changed. I made up a story for my mother when she got home, told her a purse-snatcher had scuffled with me. I couldn't tell her the truth. He was her husband. And I couldn't just run. Oh, I could have—but I wasn't of age yet, and the trust fund and the house I had inherited from my father wouldn't be mine until then. How could I live? And my mother might have guessed if I threw it all away, so I...managed. I was never again alone in the house with him; for that matter, I was rarely in the house at all." She shook her head bitterly, laughter bubbling hysterically in her throat. "The gay socialite!"

The laughter died. "It wasn't the same, going out. All the boys I'd always known and gone with before...now I would look at one and all I could see was whether or not he was stronger than I was, because whether or not he seemed nice didn't seem to matter anymore. David had always seemed very nice—too nice, too charming—and my mother used to complain that I wasn't grateful enough for his kindness."

Brian was smoothing her hair back from her forehead, a hypnotically gentle motion that she was almost unaware of, but she was beginning to be aware of the way she was nestled against him, of his arm stretched across the front of her. He had pajama bottoms on, but no top, and his chest gleamed white in the moonlight, accenting the dark patches of curling hair. She closed her eyes, suddenly exhausted. "It was over a year later that they were killed in a car crash. I dropped out from their kind of life. I made my own. I was angry with myself because I couldn't seem to get over it, couldn't stop the panic when any man but Robert touched me." She took a breath. "And then, when I was a senior in college, I met Peter." Haltingly, she described their relationship, and their break-up.

"And you believed him when he said you must be frigid. You thought that what happened with your stepfather had made you that way." His voice was strangely gritty and low.

She glanced at him, and saw that his dark eyes were fathomless and the rigidity of his expression was a denial of his gentle, soothing touch. "I don't suppose it ever occurred to you that Peter was to blame? That a more experienced, more sensitive lover might have sensed your fears, would in any case have waited until you were ready—would have known how to make you ready. I don't believe in frigid women, Leigh, only inept men."

"Poor Peter. He loved me." She hesitated, uncertain why the muscles in his chest went taut. She leaned forward suddenly, her hair swinging in a tousled curtain that covered her face. His arm followed her, his hand reaching to massage her spine. She was so emotionally exhausted that she was barely conscious. "I'm glad you don't love me," she murmured.

His fingers stilled. "What is that supposed to mean?" he demanded.

"That it would matter so much, if you cared that way," she whispered, her head bent. "I couldn't... You see, if you change your mind, you can always just leave. I'd never hold you to—"

"Red." The growl in his voice startled Leigh. "If this is your weekly offer to set me free, save it for once, would you?" Swiftly, she felt the pillows and covers being rearranged behind her.

"I just want you to understand," she started hesitantly, wearily. "Your needs may change, Brian, but mine won't, and I don't ever want you to feel tied to me."

"I have this picture of you. After it happened. Worrying about your mother and worrying about Robert, worrying about everyone around you." Firmly, he shifted her down into the cocoon of covers again, his hands possessive. "Who the hell took care of you when you needed it? All this time..." One arm folded beneath her and the other rearranged the covers to her chin, then crept under them to rest like a warm, firm weight on her rib cage. The vibrant tension in his voice had startled her, and now it suddenly disappeared. "You're never going to dream about it again, Leigh," he promised her solemnly. "You're safe, and you're going to stay that way, and right now you need to sleep."

His hand burned like fire, resting beneath the firm swell

of her breasts, but she couldn't move and could no longer even think. The release of emotions had been exhausting, and in its place was a new vulnerability that cried out for protection. Involuntarily, she moved her own hand to cover his, and his palm curled around the silk-covered breast. She felt the sudden constriction in his thighs even as the rest of his body relaxed, cradling her closer. She was aware of the current, aware that this time she had even initiated it, and aware as she had never been in her life of the intimate feel of a man's body next to hers. But it was not "a man." It was Brian—*his* hard thighs spooned under hers, *his* warm wall of chest molding to her back, *his* hand, possessive and protective. She wanted him there, beside her; she needed him. And for a single moment before she fell asleep, almost desperately, she even wanted him.

Chapter 12

TWO WEEKS LATER Leigh was standing in the dining room with a ladle in her hand, staring down into the porcelain bowl of vichyssoise. After a moment, she blinked, glanced quickly out the window, and then spooned up a dish for Robert. "Would you tell me why I made this?" she inquired of him absently. "It's supposed to be so gourmet, but all it reminds me of is gruel. I've never even liked it. *Why?*"

Robert's eyes twinkled in the chandelier's light; outside was a howling blizzard—snow hurling at the windows and wind shrieking around corners. "Because you know I like it. And so does Brian."

"Well, Brian won't be home. He's got more sense than to drive in this weather. He'll stay in town," she said firmly.

Robert shook his head. "He'll be home, Leigh." The words were barely out before the front door opened with a whistle of wind they could hear in the dining room. "See, honey?"

The lighthearted smile disappeared from her face as she

started to lay a third place for dinner. She was furious with herself for having worried about Brian for the past three hours, furious with him for driving in the blizzard. Flicking her hair back from her face, she carted the rest of the dinner to the dining room with hot pads, and by the time she took off the apron that protected her blue cotton shirtwaist, Brian was there in the doorway.

His hair was still glistening with dampness, the impassive features he'd worn since their return from Minnesota reddened by the cold. In a dark charcoal suit, he evoked the most visceral kind of sexuality. Every time he walked into a room, she felt the vibrations intensely, just as she felt the neutral mask he'd deliberately worn lately. And it hurt. It hurt like hell.

It shocked her, having to face up to how much she cared. She'd always known what he didn't want from her, just as she knew what she wasn't capable of giving him. But after Christmas—not just the release and closeness she'd felt after telling him her story, but all of it, the tenderness and sharing, his sexual teasing that one morning—she'd expected something when they got home that simply wasn't there. Had it really been just a holiday game for him, an act for his family? And her story, her sordid little story, was he now experiencing some sort of revulsion toward her because of it? Had he decided that the cool, independent woman he'd thought he'd married was in reality a hopeless neurotic? And was he merely biding his time, plotting his escape from their marriage?

She didn't want to push anything. All she really wanted, she thought fleetingly, was not to lose him. To have him in her life.

"I knew you'd make it by dinner," Robert told Brian with satisfaction. "Leigh was worried sick."

"Robert, were you one of those kids who always told tales in school?" Leigh wondered aloud as she seated herself and started passing the dishes, avoiding Brian's eyes.

"Speaking of getting into hot water, Robert, I'm about to get into a bit of some myself. With the silent redhead over here," Brian remarked.

"Don't pay any attention to her," Robert advised obligingly.

"Would the two of you rather I ate in the kitchen? Because if it's going to be one of those two-against-one nights . . ."

Brian ignored her, speaking directly to Robert. "It seems I've been roped into a two-week trip to Florida—actually, the Keys. We've been hired to submit a design for a motel complex. It's a challenging business, building anything down there. The ground's mostly coral base." He shrugged, rolling up his sleeves as he prepared to tackle the meal. "For now, it's just two weeks of discussions. But if I actually get the bid, it would mean being down there for at least two months. Actual construction might call for design changes on the spot, depending on what they find underground."

He continued to talk about the project through dinner, with Robert asking interested questions. All Leigh could think of was what it would be like without him for two weeks, much less two months or more. Perhaps he had contrived the project deliberately as a means of getting away from her.

"Well, that's all fine and good," he was saying now. "The condominium's right on the oceanfront, a good-sized place—I *hate* motels when I'm working. But I happen to need a chief cook and bottle-washer—in exchange for a spot of fun in the sun. Only redheads need apply, of course."

Leigh's eyes darted up warily, noting the glint in his eyes, directed deliberately and solely at Robert. "No," she said simply, suddenly understanding. She was not going anywhere alone with him, not again, not now that he knew. She recalled what he had said about Peter, about a more experienced, more sensitive lover. She had no intention of letting him try to "cure" her, and blow apart their whole relationship. Survival mattered, and she knew that neither she nor their marriage could survive the debacle that was certain to occur.

Brian carted his plate to the kitchen, returning with the coffeepot, still looking only at Robert. "I don't have time to cook or iron shirts. That's insulting, of course—female stereotypes and all that. And then Red's tight with a dollar, Robert; we both know that. Plane fare, a few summer clothes—we have to worry about these pennies. God knows how, between our two paltry incomes, we could scrape up a little vacation. And of course she won't want to leave *you*..."

Robert was already chuckling. "John can stay here. He cheats at cribbage, but I guess I could put up with him for a couple of weeks."

"No," Leigh repeated, still pleasantly.

"Then there's sheer bullheadedness. We're undoubtedly going to argue the advantages of slush and subzero temperatures over eighty-degree days, sunny and dry."

She opened her mouth and closed it when Robert frowned deeply at her. From Robert's viewpoint, of course, she should want to be with her husband. Leigh got up from the table, nearly tripping over the patiently waiting puppy as she took their plates to the kitchen. Monster followed, woofing politely in case she had forgotten the table scraps she wasn't supposed to give him. He woofed just as politely every night to be let out of the kitchen so he could sleep under her bed. She knelt, feeding the pup tidbits of steak, feeling a ridiculous turmoil inside. What was Brian up to now? Had she let her imagination run away with her? Maybe he did need someone to run a bit of housekeeping interference for him; but she doubted it. Maybe he felt he had to keep an eye on her because of the pregnancy. That seemed· more likely. Still...

It didn't matter why. She was vulnerable. She wanted to feel less of that, not more. She couldn't risk any more private time with Brian. "And there really isn't any other reason why he would want me to come, anyway," she whispered to the ecstatic puppy.

"Oh, yes there is, Red." He stood in the doorway, the night shadows behind him hiding the expression on his face. Startled and embarrassed, she glanced up, seeing the same night shadows in his eyes, gravely intent on hers as she drew the puppy protectively closer to her. "I need you, Leigh," he said lightly, but all of the teasing was gone from his look.

She bit on the inside of her lip, staring at him, and then bent to stroke the puppy's soft, wooly neck. How did he do it? Because she knew then that despite her misgivings and dread, she would go to the Keys with him.

*   *   *

The condominium was the opposite of what Leigh had expected. She had heard Florida was a retired man's paradise, where condos and trailer parks vied for space with tourist-attracting motels. The condominium that Brian anticipated living in for two weeks was a playboy's hideaway, with a sunken living room and creamy thick carpet throughout. A smoky-mirrored bar and hidden lighting added to the image, not to mention the master bedroom with its king-sized bed mounted on a pedestal and graced with satin sheets and a furry scarlet cover.

The place was stocked with linens and kitchenware, Leigh noted as she opened cupboards and probed corners, yet they were of a very specific kind: thick, huge towels, satin sheets; and in the kitchen there were more champagne glasses than coffee cups, cutlery and china that would gleam beautifully under candlelight, but barely enough pots to cook a proper dinner. The second bedroom stood out like a sore thumb. In harmonious blues and greens, the room had a double bed and chest in walnut, and the entire west corner was taken up by a very austere-looking drawing board and work space.

"Just your average run-of-the-mill condominium," Leigh said straight-faced to Brian, as she made a point of righting a nude print that was slightly askew on the living-room wall.

"It doesn't please?"

"Who does it belong to?" she asked, ignoring his question.

"One of the partners. It was his . . . vacation place until he married, and after that he brought it with him to the business. We've all used it at one time or another, for business reasons or not."

More "or not" Leigh thought wickedly. Good heavens, was she actually getting a sense of humor about such things?

"Leigh . . ." Brian poured his own coffee and then hers, to finish off their simple meal of steak and salad. They'd been here all of two hours. "I've got a solid week of work, and then a week that's mostly free. The Harris Company will pick me up in the morning, so you can have the rental car. Communications are going to be rough, I'm afraid. I don't imagine you're going to be inside all the time, and I don't have the least idea when I'll be home in any case."

"I can fend for myself. I had in mind burying my feet

in that carpet for at least a full morning." She simply could not raise a smile. "Go to bed, Brian. You're exhausted."

He paused. "I will. The red bedroom's yours, if you haven't already guessed. I'll need the drawing board in the other one, probably late on occasion, particularly this week."

So she was to have the bedroom with the scarlet decor, the mirrored panel on the ceiling, and the oversized, pedestaled bed. "It's not exactly my style," she said warily.

He stood up and stretched, and for almost the first time all day he smiled lazily at her. "Be a chameleon, Red. I think I'll ask you what you dreamed about in that big bed in the morning."

But Brian didn't ask; he was gone before Leigh woke up. For the next week he was just as busy as he had warned her he'd be, coming and going at odd hours, sometimes snatching meals with Leigh and sometimes just eating on the run. He came in dusty and perspiring from long hours at the proposed site. He came in frustrated and preoccupied, demanding coffee and sandwiches he never ate, and immediately retiring to his drawing board. He came in snapping and sharp, his mind knife-edged, his head full of creative ideas.

She fell in love with him that week. She loved watching him work, and she cherished the few moments that he snatched to tell her about it, to ask her opinions. The energy, thought, and sheer perseverance he put into the project astounded her. It was obviously a challenge for Brian, making something alive out of what had started out as only lead in a pencil and a vision in his head. She had not been wrong in her choice for the father of her baby. The passion, the ability to create, the instinct to see beyond obstacles and problems, the strength to order it all into being . . . that was what she wanted for her child.

For herself, it was the most wonderful vacation she'd had in an age. The coast of the Keys was fantastic: long, shallow waters, easily warmed by the sun, the coral from beneath the sea catching reflections from the sun like rainbow colors. The temperature rested just above eighty degrees, perfect for swimming, sunbathing, and combing the beaches for shells and bits of coral. Tourists of all ages sprinkled the shore, stopping to say hello if encouraged with a smile. She met people on the beaches and introduced herself to the neighbors; played tennis with one of the neighborhood boys one day, and met an old couple who went shelling with her. She was a sun child from the first day, immersing herself in every experience the time and place had to offer. Her auburn hair immediately bronzed in the sunlight, and her creamy skin honeyed with no trouble; she forgot about wearing shoes. She never felt lonely; she was too used to being really alone. On the one afternoon that it rained, she stretched lazily out on the thick carpet with a pillow and a book, ignoring the fact that she hadn't bothered to dust in a week and probably wasn't going to.

She saw Brian in passing. He left notes with phone numbers on them in case she needed anything, and she always had food prepared in case she missed his rapid passages in and out. And he did need her in his way; she understood finally why he had really wanted her to come. In his hectic schedule, there was little enough time to relax; having to freshen up and wait for service in a hotel restaurant wouldn't have suited him at all, and in a hotel that catered to vacationers there would have been no quiet place to work evenings. Nor could he be bothered about running out of clean shirts, one of his few idiosyncrasies. So she was needed, and she even gave herself silent reassurance that she was doing more for him than one of his women friends might have done. She neither demanded his time nor worried about being ignored, and she forgave his short spurts of arrogant temper because she knew they were the accompaniment of his creative genius. Most of all, she appreciated his sharing with her all his ideas and perceptions, and felt worthwhile in her role as sounding board for his innovative conceptions.

On Friday night, eight days after their arrival, Leigh heard Brian come in sometime after ten; even that early she was already in bed. She heard nothing else until the alarm clock rang for her at three-thirty in the morning. She stumbled from the bed, groping for a sweatshirt and jeans. She splashed cold water on her face, trying to fight the persistent waves of sleepiness. With her hair brushed and a windbreaker over her arm, she tiptoed through the dark hall and living room. Suddenly the light was switched on, half blinding her, and she bumped into a chair.

"Where the hell are you going?"

She whirled to face him. "Lord, I'm sorry I woke you," she said guiltily, knowing how tired he must be. His hair was rumpled boyishly, obviously fresh from sleep, and when she glanced down she saw he was barefoot. She could not ever remember actually seeing his bare feet before, which suddenly seemed very odd. She yawned. "I'll be back in a couple of hours, Brian. Go back to sleep."

"Leigh!" His voice was strangely harsh. "Where the devil are you going at four in the morning?"

"I can't quite remember; it's either shrimping or crabbing." Her sleepy eyes smiled at him disarmingly. "The Bartholomews—they're a quarter of a mile down the road, Brian. I met them on the beach—they do this all the time. They have a boat, but the tide has to be just right, and you get nets and buckets and just catch them as they flow against the current." She yawned again. "I borrowed your sweatshirt, Brian. I should have asked you, but my sweater's white and they said we might get dirty."

"And can their boat handle a fourth, Red?"

"It's huge." Her eyes widened, suddenly awake. "You actually want to go?"

"Would you rather I didn't? If these are special friends you've made . . ."

She started laughing. "It's not like that. It's just that these are hardly sophisticated people, Brian."

The Bartholomews were in their early sixties, a gray-haired couple, both of whom were plump and, like many of the condo dwellers in Florida, retired. Leigh had never seen Leonard in anything but a patched pair of shorts and a flowered shirt; and Leah was never without her straw sun hat. They took to Brian instantly, and to Leigh's surprise he took to them. Not even with his own family had she heard him laugh so much, and it was eight in the morning before they came back to their sumptuous apartment, damp and dripping, sand-encrusted, tousled, and tired. They continued to laugh as they gingerly shed their sneakers in the doorway.

"I *still* don't understand how you managed to tip over a full bucket of crabs in the middle of the boat!"

"An absolutely huge boat and your legs had to be sticking right out, taking up all the space," she retorted, giggling.

"If it hadn't been for my legs, you would have ended up in the water as well. Whoever would have thought you'd turn out to be such a sissy? Screaming bloody murder over those 'squirmy little bodies.'"

"I was not screaming." She shook her head in an expressive shudder. "If I'd known what they looked like alive, I admit I wouldn't have gone. I'll never look at another crab again for as long as I live!"

"Oh, yes, you will. Have you forgotten? First there'll be crab in the shell, then crabmeat salad. Then a round of leftovers. Then crab cocktail, boiled crab, stewed—"

"Do you think you could fancy some simple scrambled eggs for a moment?" she broke in. "Brian, do you really—truly—like crab?"

"Normally I can take it or leave it." He opened cupboards searching for the coffeepot while Leigh got out the frying pan. "At the moment, it looks as if I'll have to take it. I can't find anything in this kitchen."

"Do you expect to find the coffee in the silverware drawer? Listen, Brian, I didn't want to hurt the Bartholomews' feelings, but don't you think we could just sort of . . . slip them back into the ocean?"

There were tears in his eyes before he finished laughing. "We sat there for three solid hours, cramped and damp and salty, holding those nets in the water against the tide—what does crab cost in the store, Red, five, six dollars a pound?—and you want to sneak them back into the ocean?"

"Did I hear you say you like your scrambled eggs like leather?" Leigh asked sweetly.

"If I catch you carrying those heavy buckets all the way down to the beach edge, Red, there's going to be one part of your anatomy that will wish *it* were leather."

Silently, Leigh put the eggs on platters and brought them to the table. She returned to the kitchen for the coffeepot and juggled that with a hot pad and two cups to cart them in at the same time.

"You hear me, Leigh?"

The scrambled eggs were fascinating, and Leigh was starving. She made them with a dollop of cream cheese and a dash of chives, and it was her favorite breakfast. The bacon was crisp and the toast was blanketed with guava jelly.

"Oh, all right," Brian said impatiently.

"Thank you, Brian. Perhaps after dark, if you think they'll survive the day? The Bartholomews have a window facing the beach just like ours; I wouldn't want them to think we weren't grateful." She caught her breath at his expression. "I'm sorry," she said slowly, suddenly aware of what an absurd tantrum she'd been having, silent treatment and all— exactly the kind of thing he disliked. "It's just that I honestly don't think I could eat them, Brian, after seeing them alive. And as for killing them—"

"What are your plans for the day?" he asked abruptly.

"Laundry, beach, undoubtedly a long nap, dinner in time to stroll the beach for a sunset. But first, of course, a shower. The aroma of seaweed," she explained ruefully.

"You really haven't minded being alone so much this week, have you?" he asked bluntly.

"Did you think I expected you to hold my hand?" she said in surprise. "I'm not afraid of being alone, Brian, and there are lots of people anyway. You've been busy."

"Well, that's over now, Red, or almost over. They've got my proposals, and they've got a few days to think about them. I don't have the energy to do much today, I have to admit, but perhaps tomorrow we might rent a boat. Just cruise around, or do a bit of deep-sea fishing."

"I'd love that," she admitted softly. "That is—"

"As long as we throw back whatever we catch," he finished for her dryly.

Chapter 13

THE BOAT WAS a white, silver-streaked cabin cruiser, not so large that it couldn't be anchored in shallow waters, and not so small that there wasn't a tiny galley space and bunk-storage combined. The breeze was warm, but powerful enough to push the clouds across the horizon at a steady pace. The sun burned bright, denying its January setting, the rays dancing on the water in long, gleaming streaks as they passed. Occasionally, an island seemed to appear out of nowhere, a spot of burnished gold in the distance with perhaps a stand of scrub or palm trees or the bright color of a bird perched on a jutting rock.

Leigh had long given up the scarf she had tied on her head; there was no arguing with the wind when the boat was going full speed ahead. It didn't matter. The wind combed through to her scalp like the massage of gentle fingers, and the sensual pleasure far outweighed the instinct to preserve a neat hairdo. She closed her eyes and thought back over the last two days with Brian, a lazy blend of happy moments in her mind. They knew each other so well now; she accepted his pre-coffee growls in the morning just as he accepted the fact that stormy weather made her cross. These last days had been perfect. She had been loving him to bursting: the gentle, possessive manner he had adopted toward her, the shared laughter, his teasing, the way he looked when he came out of the water, sleek and wet.

The boat slowed and Leigh glanced toward Brian at the wheel. "Fishing time," he called down to her. For just a moment, his eyes rested on the swirling halo of her russet hair in the wind, the grace of her long, tanned limbs. "Bring up the bait box, Red."

She nodded in agreement. He had bought live shrimp as bait; the principle was to catch a decent-sized fish from them and then use that for the next bait—marlin, sailfish, baracuda. There were fish of all kinds in these deeper waters off the coast. It all sounded fine until Leigh actually opened the container. Live shrimp bore no resemblance at all to the shrimp she'd eaten in a restaurant: orange and squirmy, with tiny beady eyes and tentacles worse than a tarantula's. She glanced back at Brian, who was standing behind her putting together the poles and already set to laugh at her.

"Besides, that's an inhuman way to die," she pointed out. "Stabbed viciously on a hook and in pain for hours, unless it's lucky enough to have some terrifying thing come up and eat it for lunch."

"So you want me to bait your hook for you, Red?" Brian said, straight-faced.

"No way."

She baited her hook with bologna stolen from her sandwich, glaring at Brian when he laughed and refusing to even look at his pole until his shrimp was under the water. Prepared for a long siege of waiting, she was startled when only a few minutes later she felt a strong jerk on her line that tugged her to a standing position.

"It's *huge!*" She needed both of her hands to hold the pole. For minutes the line went slack and then suddenly the fish pulled again, jerking her off-balance with its surprising strength.

"I don't want to disillusion you, Red, but the chances

of catching a shark with two inches of bologna are absolutely nil."

"Sour grapes, Mr. Hathaway. And you said I wouldn't catch anything!" They had to half-shout at each other over the stiff breeze. Leigh was giggling like a child at the triumph of her first catch. "Quit fighting!" she called out over the white-tipped waters. "You'll only hurt yourself! I'll let you go as soon as I can!"

The line jerked stiffly, bringing Leigh halfway to her feet again. She struggled for balance, trying to pin the rod between her legs for added support so she could reel it in.

"You *could* ask for help," pointed out Brian.

"This is *my* fish!" she protested, breathless from her efforts. The strap of her suit slipped from her shoulder; her hands were almost trembling with the effort of holding the line. With a puzzled frown, Brian was scanning the waters for her prey. Then he sighted it. "Damn it, Red, what the hell have you got there?"

The next minutes were a confusing kaleidoscope in her mind. Brian taking care of his own line and coming up behind to help her; laughter; her playful insistence that she *would* handle it when she was increasingly disgruntled to find she couldn't; then his hand circling her waist, bolstering her back to the cradle of his hard thighs—only to give her support, she didn't doubt that, so she could reel the line in on her own. But then her mind registered something else. He was all but naked, and so was she. She saw her breast peaking out from where the bathing strap had slipped, felt the strength in his legs and chest, naked and hot. The scent was there: sun, salt, man. Heat and power. It had happened so fast. She would trust him with her life; it wasn't that. It was just the old instinctive dread, and in the confusion she prayed he wouldn't notice that her heart was racing. If he didn't release her soon...

He didn't seem to notice. It was natural to separate as they both surveyed their unexpected haul. The fish was reddish-orange, scaly and fat, perhaps three feet in length and almost as wide as it was long. Its gold eyes stared sightlessly, and its gills heaved as it tried desperately to escape. The fish took up most of the floor space on the slippery deck.

"Brian, he's going to die if we don't get him back in the water," Leigh said worriedly.

"Is that *all* you can say?"

She loved the curve of his smile, felt relief flow through her body like warm honey. "I certainly hope he enjoyed the bologna."

Brian laughed as he knelt down to free the hook from the fish's mouth. "It's the biggest snapper I've ever seen. Look, Red."

Cautiously, she angled closer. The bologna had not caught the snapper. A smaller fish, brown and speckled, had gone for the sandwich meat; the hook had erupted through the skin of its mouth and caught the snapper when it unwisely went after the live bait.

"I've never seen anything like that."

"If I'd just waited a little longer," Leigh said artlessly, "we could probably have gotten the shark that went for the snapper."

"A fish story, if ever I've heard one!"

"Gee, how's your shrimp doing, Brian? Any bites?"

It was easy to joke and laugh again, to pretend the moment of fear had never existed. No small amount of perspiration and swearing and effort—on Brian's part—later, and the fish was back in the water. It plunged deep and Leigh held her breath; then she chuckled again. The snapper was not so hurt that it was not willing and able to be instantly on its way.

She and Brian shared a drink and snack, and then mutually agreed that any more immediate exercise was out of the question. Instead, they made their way to the front of the boat to put down their towels. Brian stretched out full length on his back; Leigh wanted to believe she was more comfortable sitting with her knees drawn up, that his closeness was not affecting her again. She closed her eyes, listening. The water slop-slurped against the sides of the boat in a lulling rhythm, and the sounds of gulls were suddenly pervasive—a haunting, piercing series of cries as they fished for their prey. Peaceful. She could almost lose herself in the mesmerizing music of water and birds; in the warmth of the sun and the hypnotic rocking.

"Lie back, Leigh."

Her eyes blinked open. She knew in an instant that he had been aware of her earlier reaction to him. Helplessly, she wondered if he could sense the shiver of fear that ran through her now at the tone of his voice. He had given an order, an order he intended her to obey, an order wrapped in the deep, silky texture of his seductive voice.

She lay on her side, careful to face away from him, staring out over the waters at the clouds like carelessly painted splotches on the horizon. A storm was building. The colors of the sky were blending with those of the sea at the curve of the horizon, a mixture of purples and grays. Overhead, the sun still burned brightly, the intensity so great that it sapped energy from the body.

Her tension relaxed and was instantly recharged as his palm roamed over the back of her legs, soothing suntan lotion on them in long, sure strokes. Slowly, from her calf to the back of her thigh to the fabric of her suit. A moment of hesitation, and then from the other thigh down to her calf, to the slim, strangely sensitive circle of her ankle. There wasn't a nerve ending in her body that hadn't tightened at his caressing touch. His sensuous touch. She knew he could feel in his hands the muscles that went helplessly taut; but he was ignoring it.

The tiny suit straps were slipped from her arms, and his hands started working on her back and shoulders. As fast as she built up tension, he was working to erase it, not allowing any knots or stiffness. He knew too much, taking her flesh in his hands as if it were putty, his fingers sneaking in beneath the fabric of her suit, warm, vibrant, insistent. Her skin sang with the heat. She desperately wanted to move away, but couldn't. The foreboding was there, and something she didn't want to believe. He was writing novels with his touch. Mysteries. Her heart didn't know whether to beat fast or slow, but she knew with every instinct that he wanted her.

"Flip onto your back," he said quietly.

"No, Brian." It was only a whisper, barely audible.

"Turn over, Leigh." That tone again.

Helplessly, she said nothing, and after a moment she heard a growl of annoyance. With firmness and confidence, he reached for her waist and shoulder to turn her over himself. Her body reacted rather than her mind: her fingers became claws, intent on self-preservation; her feet skidded on the deck, intent on escape. The water simply reached out to her, and she jumped with her hands protectively over her stomach, too panicked even to remember to hold her breath. Her foot touched bottom and something sharp and painful pierced the sole. The water felt unpleasantly icy to Leigh's sun-fevered skin. Something slithery brushed her leg, and in horror she swallowed a mouthful of salt water, gasping and choking as she finally surfaced.

"Brian!"

It took time for Brian to drive the boat back to its rental place, time to snatch a carry-out dinner, time to drive back home to the condominium. Brian came around to her side of the car, opened her door, and scooped her up in his arms, carting her wordlessly through the apartment until they'd reached her bedroom and the massive pedestaled bed. Leigh felt like an absolute fool. Her foot had been badly cut and it smarted; her tongue refused to make a reasonable effort at conversation; and the last few hours of wretchedly silent tension between them had started a pounding headache in her temples. Making matters even worse was the fact that the discomfort seemed to be on her part. Brian's only re-action to her escapade had been to mildly call her an idiot and point out that the baby might not have appreciated the premature baptism. She had thought—she had been *sure*— that there was fury in his eyes when he hauled her out of the water, but his later manner and tone had denied it, and that first show of emotion had been quickly masked.

Almost brusquely he deposited her on the furry scarlet bedspread. "All right, Red. I know you better than to forbid you the shower—you'll be determined to get the salt water out of your hair—but I don't want you to put any weight on that foot. Understand? Coral has a way of effecting some people like poison."

Indifferently, he surveyed her, his glance taking in Leigh, the bed, the sensuous furnishings of the scarlet bedroom. He had not been in there before, not even once. His manner was unfathomable. She wanted desperately to offer him an apology, to bring back the warm, easy laughter. His detachment over the last two hours had been exactly as it was when he first met her; exactly, at one time, all she'd wanted from him.

He was gone before she could tender the apology; at any rate, she did not know what to say. Listlessly, she got off the bed again and hobbled into the bath, stripping off the damp, salty suit and the sweatshirt she had borrowed from him. The shower stung her body in hot torrents like a punishment; her foot stung, too, where it had been cut, and she noticed an unsightly bruise on her thigh, gotten heaven knew where in that escapade.

At last the sticky salt was washed from her hair and she emerged into the foggy bathroom, flushed and clean. Wrapping herself in one of the huge bath towels, she perched on the counter to avoid standing, and dried and brushed her hair. When that was done, she reached for her short terry wrap and used the towel to wipe the fog from the mirrors— it was crazy to do an entire wall of a bathroom in mirrored tiles—and found herself staring at her reflection. The white wrap was a startling contrast to the warm honey color of her skin. Her hair curled softly at the shoulders; a burnished swathe waved sensually over one eye, and she brushed it aside in an automatic gesture. Brown eyes stared back at her, oval with the faintest hint of an upward slant, brooding, intense, sensitive. How *could* she have acted so foolishly on the boat? More important, how could she ever have let herself fall in love with Brian when she knew how she was?

Abruptly, Leigh turned away. She shivered when she opened the door and was met with the startling contrast of temperatures. The bedroom was cool and shuttered during the day, and after the neon brightness of the bathroom she had to blink once or twice to accustom herself to the dimmer light.

"Brian!"

His dark form was stretched out on the bed, thoroughly relaxed, thoroughly at home, and Leigh thoughtlessly put weight on the ball of her cut foot in an unconscious movement backward, wincing as she did so.

"I'm here to take a good look at that, Red." He had showered, too, she noticed. His hair was like a black helmet,

still damp, framing the austere features of his face. Wearing
only thin navy cords, he was barefoot and bare-chested, and
when he moved to get off the bed, she could see the rippling
of muscles across his chest and shoulders.

"No more Mercurochrome," she said warily, still standing in the same spot. Not for anything would she allow
herself to run again, or even to think of running. But the
awareness was there once more, intensified by the knowledge that she had nothing on beneath the white terry-cloth
wrap, the awareness that she was alone with this sensual,
magnetic husband of hers.

He jerked the spread and blankets from their neat folds
on the bed. "Lie on your stomach with your head at the
bottom of the bed," he suggested. She understood when he
switched on the high-intensity lamp and angled the bulb so
that it would shine on the base of her foot. But as for getting
under the sheets, there seemed no point in that, no point in
being imprisoned by covers. Brian was staring at her.
"Somehow I thought you'd be more comfortable covered.
Unless you're wearing a full dress uniform under that."

She flushed, and hurried to do as he said. "You make
this sound like an operation," she tried to joke.

"It may be. Mercurochrome was all we could do on the
boat, Red, but it's a damned deep cut. We've got to make
sure you haven't got any coral imbedded in there." His tone
was as impersonal as a stranger's; he flipped the blanket
over her back, sat down by the headboard, and put her foot
in his lap. The lamp was hot on the sole of her foot and his
touch sure. His fingers felt warm and dry.

"So, will I live?" she finally asked.

"It looks clean enough. A bit wrinkled," he said dryly.
"You like your showers hot, don't you? This is going to
sting."

She didn't flinch, though it did burn.

"So you *can* be brave on occasion?" There was something
different about him tonight; he was familiar and yet strange
in a way Leigh couldn't understand. "Now just close your
eyes and relax for a minute. Let it dry. The air should be
better than a bandage for it until morning."

He put her foot down and rose. "Just stay there." Sounds
rustled at the head of the bed; he was putting away the first-

aid supplies. He diverted the lamp glare so that it made a circle of light on the carpet.

"Are your eyes closed?" he asked quietly.

"Is this all part of the healing process, doctor?" she asked wryly, but she closed her eyes. She was exhausted and the sheets felt soft and soothing beneath her; she was warm again. She must have lain there several minutes under the pretext of waiting for the disinfectant to dry.

The covers shifted from the opposite side of the bed, letting in a draught of cool air. A flutter pulse in her throat threaded out a sudden uneven beat. She opened her eyes and started to get up. Brian was there, waiting. Not urgently, he caught hold of her arms, and losing her leverage she fell back on the silken sheets. The terry robe had loosened, and as he leaned over her to keep her wrists firmly pinned on the mattress, his bare chest brushed her own. His flesh was shockingly cool and almost bristly next to her soft white breasts; one heartbeat hovering over another. Leigh went rigid, feeling disbelief and betrayal as she stared at him accusingly.

His eyes never left hers. For all the firmness of his grip, he was not hurting her, but simply forcing her to remain still. "It's past time, Leigh," he said softly. "You've had years to put your ghosts to rest. You've no business letting them spoil your life. Your fear is real; I know that. But you haven't even experienced the emotions you think you're afraid of. You're not afraid of making love; you don't even know what it is. What happened with Peter was a . . . mistake. Do you hear me?"

She shook her head perversely, a hint of tears accenting her vulnerability. She was rigid and trembling violently at the same time, and she couldn't seem to remember how to breathe properly.

"You understand?" He denied her head-shaking. "You know I won't hurt you, Leigh." His voice was like raw silk. He kissed her eyes shut. "Fight, Leigh. It's all right. Anything you do is all right," he whispered. "But we're going past that fear, Leigh."

"You promised," she whispered, opening her eyes wide. "Don't. Please, Brian. Please."

In answer, the weight of his chest increased, and her

wrists were released when she was pinned by his body itself. With infinite gentleness, his hands reached up to tangle in her hair, his fingers cradling her head. His lips touched hers, teasing and light. Once more he kissed her lids closed, and then he kissed the faint salty dampness of tears on her cheeks. Smooth and warm, his mouth trailed a slow erotic path down her neck, taking a year to do it, learning everything there was to learn along the way as if he had decades to devote to just the skin of her face and neck.

Leigh was utterly still for a long time, her eyes closed. As consuming as the fear was, she felt other sensations that contradicted the instinct to flee. And somehow she didn't move in that single moment when she could have, those seconds when he removed his pants and was not holding her with both hands. Then his weight shifted back to her, and she felt the graze of his thighs as he slid lower, one of his legs nudging apart hers. His head nuzzled the material of her robe to open it further. There was a moment when he didn't touch, when she knew he was just looking. The sight of breasts—how many dozens had he seen?—but he treated them as if he'd never known anything so lovely. His head dipped; his lips brushed back and forth on the firm satin flesh, light sensual flicks of his tongue heated and cooled. The nipples swelled and stiffened beneath his touch. It shocked her, her reaction to the feel of his lips on her breasts, the betrayal from within.

Betrayal . . . She moved then, suddenly, desperately, writhing to get free. She kicked out, shaking the covers off, frantically trying to kick him. Wild, uncontrollable tremors coursed through her body. "Easy, easy, Leigh . . ." She heard the tone, the gentleness out of nowhere, just as she felt the firm, sure touch of him, controlling, not hurting. She shot up a knee; his hand was waiting for it. Her teeth grazed his shoulder but could not connect. And still, his words kept coming, soft and sure: "I *know*, Leigh . . . a little fight, love. A little. To let it out . . . sooner or later you'll stop fighting. I'm your husband, Leigh, and I'm not going to hurt you. No matter what you do . . . it's all right, Leigh."

"I hate you!" Tears streamed from her eyes. And yet surging through her bloodstream was a terrifying instinct to just let go. "I hate you," she repeated desperately, pinned beneath his hard, virile body. Helplessness was an emotion she couldn't handle, would never again be able to handle.

For hours, it seemed, she found herself staring up at him, her breath still coming in frantic little pants, consumed by bitterness, and exhaustion from that brief struggle. Her breath came normally after a time, but the trembling from the contact with him would not cease. He saw. Damn it, he saw. She could see it in his eyes, that he didn't believe in her hate, and that nothing she said was going to make any difference. His palm softly traced the line of her cheek, smoothed back her hair. His gentleness . . . Like a pent-up dam she had the terrifying feeling she was about to explode, yet she couldn't seem to move, and she was held in those black depths of his eyes, mesmerized.

"Now we'll try, Leigh," he whispered.

"It won't work. Please, Brian . . ." Yet her whole body burned when his mouth pressed on hers, when his hands started caressing. Every place he touched, a fire of rage and desire was ignited. Leigh felt confused, humiliated. Still her lips yielded to the searing pressure, to the probing soft-ness of his tongue. Such power in his hands, such terrifying power! He cradled her hips against his, rubbing a tension to the sudden silk dampness of her skin that she felt like a cry inside of her. She couldn't breathe; he just wouldn't stop to let her breathe, and the wildness inside threatened to split her apart.

A volcano of hurts was trying to bubble over, free itself. One minute she was feverishly kissing him back, responding from her soul, and the next she was struggling again, frozen and terrified. The waiting was unbearable. If it could just be *over;* but instead the heat kept building, along with an aching that echoed like pain.

And then Brian took over. "Softer now, lady," he whis-pered raggedly. In slow motion, his hands explored every hollow, every crevice, every plane of her body. His mouth pressed relentlessly on hers, demanding her commitment. His eyes were like dark glass in the muted light; they loved her, caressed her, were as involved in her every reaction as she herself was. He nurtured her awakening passion as if it were a live thing newly born—nurtured, fed, encouraged, comforted.

The commitment was given. Her back arched, straining to him. Soft whimpers escaped from her lips. She whispered his name over and over, pleading with him as he continued to stroke and caress her most intimate places. She felt his leg push hers open, his hands tangle in her hair, and then his mouth came down on hers to swallow that shock as his body melted into hers. To her surprise, the discomfort was negligible. Her body was treacherously ready for him, opened to him like a flower, and a wetness she hadn't known was there smoothed his entry into her flesh. Their bodies joined, but he didn't move yet, combing his fingers through her hair, planting sweet, encouraging kisses on her forehead, her cheeks, her lips.

At last he shifted, asking so tenderly that she go with him, his body moving slowly, then faster as she took up the rhythm. Her fears seemed to evaporate as she strained to stay with him, crying, exhilarated, somehow knowing exactly what he wanted, somehow craving the identical motion herself. Flame turned to fire; tinder exploded. She cried out; then he did.

Leigh's body shuddered in relief, in wonder. She had never dreamed it could be like that, still couldn't believe the beauty, the joy of it. Brian held her for a long time afterward, caressing her still, pressing his lips to her forehead over and over as if he were calming a child. And then that passed, too. She pressed her cheek to his shoulder, feeling strangely embarrassed and shy.

"Bashful? Well, you should be," he teased gently. "If that's your definition of frigid, Red, I think it's time they rewrote Webster's."

He finally removed his arms, got out of the bed, and stretched, grinning at her like a Cheshire cat. "Don't go away."

Naked, he strode from the room, returning a few minutes later with a glass of wine for himself and grape juice for her, ruby-colored in the soft light. "Did you know it was midnight?"

She shook her head mutely. Shock was beginning to set in, shock that the entire world had gone right side up in such a short time—love and shyness and an indescribable

sense of wonder. And Brian was so casually sorting through
the bedclothes, setting the pillows comfortably behind them,
tucking the covers around her to ward off the chill of the
night.

"It's your own fault, lady. I'd had enough of your jump-
ing at the touch of a fingertip; I'll admit that. And I'll admit
that I wasn't going to let you go until you responded, and
I shook you out of that shell you'd enclosed yourself in.
You damned near could have killed yourself today, and I
barely laid a finger on you on the boat. But that was all I
intended, Leigh. I would never have forced you to go any
further. You forced that issue yourself. Although if I'd known
you had that sort of fire underneath . . ." He handed her the
glass, toasting her as he did so, his black eyes sparkling
with mischief.

"Brian . . . I . . . Thank you," she murmured inade-
quately.

"Thank *you*," he responded vibrantly. His exuberance
faded with a sigh that recalled the long and eventful hours
of the day. He tucked his arm around her shoulder, and
sipped his wine. "Are you hurting, Red?" he asked huskily.

Unbearably. Hurting with a feeling of love for him, so
intense and complete that she didn't know quite what to do
with it. But she knew that wasn't what he meant. "No, not
at all," she murmured, and added quietly, "I'm sorry, Brian.
If I hurt you when I was—"

Almost roughly he kissed her with wine-flavored lips.
"You took a long time in the persuading, love, but then the
sort of fears you've been living with aren't easily erased.
And I don't expect they are now, altogether—but they will
be."

Her eyes widened at the implication that this was not to
be a one-time occurrence. She hadn't even thought of that,
and she didn't want to now. She had encountered a new
kind of fear during their lovemaking. A fear of being mas-
tered, of losing oneself entirely in the possession of another.
It was a delicious and dangerous feeling, and had added to
the thrill of the passion itself.

But it was the feeling of love that had turned the tide,
born of his possession, his power over her, his incredible

tenderness. She had responded to the concern she felt in him, a concern far more potent and powerful than her fear. That was what had bridged the years of fears, of memories. Not just passion, but passion in loving. But she didn't know how to tell him that.

Chapter 14

THE OTHER SIDE of the bed was empty when Leigh awoke. It was nine o'clock, yet still she burrowed deeper into the covers for a few minutes. Last night . . .

She closed her eyes again, savoring the warm memories that washed over her. Never would she have believed she could forget the pain and degradation she had suffered at her stepfather's hands, that she would be free to experience the depth and wealth of loving she had found with Brian. He had taken away her choices the night before, but given her back one she had never expected: the simple and fierce desire to give of herself, the need to give, the right to love. And she did love him. It wasn't just the sexual passion, but so many things she could think back on now and see where she had been afraid to admit her own feelings. Even from the very beginning, she thought ruefully, she had been drawn to this man she wanted as the father of her child, the man she would choose again tomorrow and tomorrow and tomorrow.

Leigh stretched luxuriantly, feeling alive and warm and whole. But suddenly a disquieting thought struck her. Her world had turned upside down overnight, but there was no reason to think that Brian's had. Brian wanted no love; he saw passion as a physical need, and emotional commitment as a burden. He had never said anything to indicate that his feelings had changed—except his sexual feelings for her. She shivered suddenly, bitterly aware of the terms they'd set for the marriage. How many times had she promised him he could get out whenever he wanted? That she would never tie him down, become clingingly attached to him?

"Hey, lazy one. You've been squandering the whole morning away!" With a tray in his hands, Brian used his foot to kick open the door. Scrambled eggs with a faintly scorched aroma and a platter of toast was set before her, as she sat up in bed.

There was enough for two but only one tray, and she really did have to laugh at him. More crumbs ended up on the bed than in either of their mouths, and he hadn't lied when he said he was no cook.

He grimaced at the taste of the rubbery eggs. "It wasn't my fault. The toast had the nerve to come up just when the eggs were done, and then I had to butter that before it got cool. I thought I'd turned the eggs down, but instead I'd turned them up."

She laughed, forgetting her worries. "It's delicious, Brian," she soothed him. "Don't you know that everything tastes delicious when you don't have to cook it?"

"I don't know if I like the sound of that. I was rather hoping you'd lock me out of the kitchen forever." He talked on. They had one more full day, and then it was back to work for Brian. Wednesday he had invited the Harrises and their wives and John White for cocktails, to hear their decision on his proposals. Phil and Dan Harris were the owners and John White the potential manager of the complex. They were as difficult to deal with as any clients Brian had ever had. But the commission was excellent, and wintertime commissions of any kind were rare. With the state of the economy as it was . . .

Although Leigh was interested and listening, her attention kept returning to his eyes, which reminded her of the stone called Apache's tears—black, with a particular luminescent quality that gave an illusion of transparency.

"So, lady, shower and do your stuff, and I'll bandage that foot of yours, and we'll be off." He disappeared with the tray, and Leigh quickly scrambled out of bed, gathering her clothes together as she headed for the bathroom. Her spirits were soaring, but was this the way it was to be? Talking so easily, being pampered, teased—but what did it all mean? Was he this way with every woman he made love with, especially the first time?

Abruptly, she put these anguished thoughts behind her. One more full day with him; she would let nothing disturb her. Not yet... The shower was refreshing, tingling on her skin. She was only under the hot spray a minute when she felt a cold rush of air as the bathroom door opened. "Brian?"

There was no answer, and she thought she had imagined it. Then the glass shower door was opened, and wordlessly he stepped in with her, naked and tall. She might have smiled if he had been smiling; just a few minutes ago they had been talking so easily. But he was not smiling now. His dark eyes bored into hers, his intent unmistakable. She didn't move, but there was a sudden frantic feeling clutching at her heart. Until he touched her...

"That's why," he said. "That's why, Leigh. I don't want you to think, not just yet." He lathered the soap in his hands, smoothing it first over her back and neck, lingering over her hips and thighs before he turned her around. Slowly, deliberately, he slid his soapy palms from her throat to her breasts, then down her ribs to the soft mound of her stomach, his eyes intently watching her reactions. "We made the baby last night, you know," he whispered. "Not before."

"I wasn't thinking about the baby last night," she admitted breathlessly.

"I was. It wasn't real until then. Not for me."

Very gently, he raised her arms and laced them around his neck. His body was slippery when he molded her to him, and the stream of water on her back beat a rhythmic, sensual tattoo. The blood rushing through her veins remembered the wonder of the night before; the erratic pulse in her throat remembered years before. She raised her face instinctively to his, pleading with him. His lips dipped on hers, savoring the softness she offered, and desperately she clung, holding on as his kiss deepened in fire, arching her throat back. She had the crazy sensation that she would drown if he let her go, that last night would disappear and the fear consume her as it always had.

But he did not let her go. There was no patient, slow lovemaking this time. His hands had their own fever, which he transferred to her flesh wherever he touched; his mouth was hungry for the taste and feel of her. She could not breathe, suddenly, could not get enough of his warm, slippery skin against hers, could not bear the slow, insidious curl of need inside her, so raw, so sweet, so fierce.

She had only a vague memory of getting out of the shower, of being dried and then cradled in a towel. She remembered being pressed into cool sheets by the weight of his body; remembered the husky growl in his throat when she touched him . . . and kept on touching him. He had demanded nothing of her the night before, but now, she felt he was demanding everything—her body and soul. And she had it to give; he made it so easy. She cried out when his body blended with hers, not in pain but in the unbelievable joy of it. It was impossible to believe there could be anything wrong when his arms were around her. He was all tenderness again when it was over, murmuring endearments, soothing her trembling with soft kisses and velvet strokes.

For long minutes of silence, his arms enclosed her, protecting her. At last her heartbeat returned to normal, and she gazed up at his face, trying to read what he was feeling. He looked sleepy with his eyes half-shuttered, but he had a knack for keeping secrets, and suddenly she knew she could not just let it be. "Brian? Why did you make love to me?"

His eyes flickered open, then traveled over her body from head to toe, returning playfully to her eyes. "How much detail do you want in that answer?" he teased, his voice husky.

She shook her head, unhappy with his banter. "You never wanted me before," she said softly.

"I wanted you from the first moment I saw you in my office with your hair loose and your glasses off. I wanted you even more—desperately—that night at your house when

I saw you standing in that white robe of yours against the firelight."

She gave him a startled look, then got out of bed.

"You couldn't have," she said stiffly as she bent to find clothes in the drawers. "You made it very clear that you couldn't care less!"

Brian leaned back against the pillows, studying her. She could feel him watching as she slipped on a pair of panties and then more quickly drew on a summery shift of emerald green. "I had no intention of breaking faith with you then, Red, if that's what you're asking," he said quietly, the teasing note disappearing from his voice. "The opposite was true. I wanted a wife I could live with on my terms, and I was too eager to believe I had found one to push for something you so clearly didn't want. That was what you had in mind, wasn't it? For me to take care of all physical needs outside of this marriage of ours?"

She turned uncertainly. "Yes, that was what I had in mind," she said defensively, staring with an odd feeling of lifelessness at the golden skin of his shoulders, naked above the carelessly tossed sheet. But when her gaze moved up a few inches, he caught her look and held it with his own. The starkness of honesty was suddenly there, in the charcoal depths of his eyes.

"You weren't who you said you were. That shell of protection you built around yourself was just that—a shell. Someone, sometime, was going to break through it, hopefully before you'd built up too many more layers. By all rights it should have been a man you loved, a man you intended and really wanted to spend your life with. By all rights," he repeated almost harshly, "it should not have been me."

"Brian . . ." she said unhappily.

He shook his head, denying her interruption. "I didn't forget about those rights, Leigh. But I deliberately put them aside. I wanted you, and I was certain I could reach you last night. More important than any of that was that I wouldn't hurt you, and when I started to think about the wrong kind of man getting hold of you again, Leigh, I couldn't stand the thought of adding to the scars you already had. Whether you believe it or not, it wasn't for myself that I made love

to you last night... at least in the beginning," he admitted
with just a touch of dryness in his voice. "But once you
took fire..." he smiled at the sudden flush that softened
her cheeks. "And I have to confess that good intentions had
nothing to do with this morning. You just looked so damned
beautiful lying in that bed with your hair all tumbled and
toast crumbs on your breasts."

"I..." But she hadn't anything to say. She just watched
as he drew back the sheet and stood up, his sleek, tanned
body totally natural in nakedness.

His tone was brisk when he spoke again. "I'd like to
regret breaking a promise, Leigh, but I don't. And if you
want to go back to the old arrangement, I will. It's up to
you entirely whether you want to share a bed. I won't force
you, and I won't play any seduction games."

He faced her, waiting. Her answer came out easily before
she even thought. "Brian, I love you," she said simply.

She thought she saw a strange flicker in his eyes before
he put on his neutral mask. He picked up the towel from
the floor and draped it around his waist, then approached
her, brushing back her hair and resting his palms on both
sides of her neck. "You don't have to say that, Leigh. And
I won't hold you to it. You're feeling good about yourself.
You've become a whole woman, and I was around for the
transition. There's no harm in calling it love for now, but
you won't call it that later." His brows were furrowed together, but his mouth curved in a smile. "Shall we just let
it be?"

She felt a lump in her throat almost like clotted tears.
"Is that what you want?" she asked quietly.

"The reason we're talking is to determine what *you* want,"
he said sharply.

But was it? she wondered.

Don't bring love into it was what she understood him to
be telling her. Don't love me, because I don't love you.
Actually, it was what she'd expected from him; he had never
lied to her about his feelings. She took a breath and managed
to look up at him with a bright smile that masked her inner
pain. "That's rather a major decision to make on the spur
of the moment. I mean, one single night isn't proof that

you don't snore, or steal all the covers in the early part of
the morning, or—"

Swiftly, his lips covered hers, and she responded, feeling
as soft as buttercups inside, relieved to have answered him
the way he evidently wanted, lightly. Inside, she thought
fleetingly that perhaps in time . . . But she didn't have much
time to look her best for him. All too soon, her figure would
be gone as the child within her grew; and even now, three
and a half months pregnant, she was a long way from the
svelte women he had been photographed with in the past.

"Lord, you weigh a ton!"

"Just put me down then," Leigh protested. She was hoisted
on Brian's shoulders as they trudged back to the condominium from the beach. The sun had set hours ago, and it
was just that many hours since they had started walking. In
the beginning, Leigh had been conscious of her sore foot,
but not so much that she would forgo this outing on the
beach with her husband: the sunset, the moonlit stroll. By
the time she was unable to avoid limping, they were far
from home . . . too far for her to make it back on her own,
as Brian had realized all too rapidly. "Just put me down,"
she repeated.

"No. There's a slim chance that I could learn to like
suffering."

She chuckled, glancing up. All day they had ridden along
the coast, stopping to rest or snack as it suited them. All
day there had been wind and blustery skies, but that had
changed early in the evening. The moonlight was bright,
reflecting silver on the long stretches of sand. A black ocean
was indistinguishable from the night sky except for the flashes
of white-tipped waves. The sound of the surf seemed eternal,
coming from all around the blackness, hypnotic and ro-
mantic. They had stopped more than once for a kiss, occasionally for more than a kiss.

A short while later, they reached the condominium.
Brian's arms reached up, grasped her waist, and she was
rather unceremoniously hauled over his head and placed on
the doorstep. He flexed his shoulders in exaggerated com-

plaint, and she opened the door with a smile, hobbling in ahead of him.

"So you think I've gained a little weight lately?" she asked teasingly.

"A *little?*"

"Don't you think you're making an awful lot out of a hundred and fifteen pounds? If you think of it in terms of carrying at least two of us . . ."

"Want anything?" He wandered to the bar, switching on the recessed lighting as he did so. "And what's that supposed to mean—'*At least* two'?"

"No thanks. These pants are wet at the hems, Brian. I'm going to change."

"I am, too. It's late." He switched the lighting off again, and with an ice-filled drink in his hand followed her down the hall, hesitating at the doorway of the scarlet bedroom. "What do you mean—'at least two'?" he asked again impatiently.

Leigh took a nightgown and robe into the bathroom. "My dad was a twin," she called from there, "although my uncle died before I ever met him. And Dad's dad was a twin, too, although I never met him either. It was hard enough getting together with my grandfather—he lived in San Francisco. Died a year after my dad did." She emerged from the bathroom, her hair newly brushed and a powder-blue robe wrapped around her.

"Leigh, why didn't you mention the possibility of twins when you first came to my office?" He stood still, leaning against the doorjamb, very much the forbidding stranger she had first met many months ago. Mechanically, she moved to the pedestaled bed and slowly pulled down the scarlet cover in careful folds.

"It's not really all that likely," she said placatingly. "A little more than for most people."

"You should have told me before we made our visit to the doctor."

She did not want to argue with him. She turned on a lamp and slipped in on the side of the monstrously huge bed, reaching for the book on the nightstand. "One or two or ten didn't matter then," she said in a deliberately soothing tone. "All that mattered was that together we could produce a healty child, that what gifts I could give it through inheritance—"

"Which twins are. An inherited trait."

She opened the book with a cross expression for him. "I meant important things: health, intelligence—"

"There's an additional risk to your life, isn't there, with twins? Complications are more common. The pregnancy can be more difficult. Coping afterwards is *obviously* more difficult."

"Women rarely die in childbirth anymore," she replied. "The birth of twins is often quicker and easier because the babies are smaller than average. I'm a very healthy lady, Brian"

"I can't believe you would conceal the possibility of twins from me," he said harshly.

His accusing tone struck her as unreasonable, but deeper than that she felt a chill inside at the sudden breach between them. "Brian, if you're angry because you feel that twins would be an additional burden on you, please don't worry," she said. "I knew from the beginning that children didn't fit into your lifestyle; we both did. And I knew from the beginning, I think . . . that this marriage wouldn't suit you forever. You want freedom, a peaceful home. That isn't what a household with a baby is about. If you hadn't already planned on leaving when the child was born—"

"Who said anything about leaving?" he broke in. "For that matter, where did you come up with the notion that I don't like children?" he said furiously. "Did you see me beat my nephews and nieces at Christmas?"

"No," she admitted, with a wary smile. "But that's not the same thing as having a child around all the time, one you can't escape from." She hesitated. She had thought, all day, about the two of them. The more she loved him, the less she could accept his staying with her out of a sense of responsibility.

He leaned over the bed, pulling back the covers from her lap. She clung stubbornly to the book in her hand. "Damn it," he said wryly. "It's not easy for you to give up an ounce of independence, is it? You're so damned stubborn."

"I am not. You make it sound so . . . I just want you to

understand that you don't have to feel trapped."

He chuckled, the last of the chill in his expression softening. "Idiot, Red. Come on." He took the book from her hands and switched off the light. "This mattress is too soft. Mine's better, and it'll be a lot easier to find you in the middle of the night besides."

So she was sleeping with him? It certainly hadn't felt like that a moment ago. Rather nervously, she slipped her legs over the side and stood up, glancing covertly at him. They were married; married people slept together. But they were hardly a typical married couple, and she didn't have any idea what the rules were after the night before. "If you're still angry," she started hesitantly.

"Furious," he corrected lazily as he prodded her toward the doorway. "And if you have any other tidbits of medical information you've failed to pass on, you'd better do it now."

She shook her head, smiling softly as they walked down the hall to his room. "There's nothing."

"How I would like to believe you," he said ironically, "but somehow, Red, you've been throwing me nothing but curveballs from the first time I laid eyes on you."

Without switching on the light, he moved ahead of her to draw down the spread and blankets. She slipped in, with her head toward the window as she heard him take off his clothes. In the darkness, she could feel it, an electrical charge, a rush, as if all day her blood had been sluggish and was suddenly racing. She felt an acute sense of shyness, mixed with anticipation.

His weight depressed the mattress next to her. He leaned over her, his palm gently covering her violent heartbeat and then gliding up to her chin as he pressed a gentle kiss on her lips. "No, Red," he whispered. "Tell that pulse of yours that one of us is new at this game."

"What?" She reached up, her fingertips tracing the line of his jaw, already mesmerized by the softness of his eyes in the dark.

"You need your rest," he said firmly. Gently, he removed her exploring fingers, curling her back to the mold of his chest, and settled in like a man seeking rest.

It was . . . interesting, she thought vaguely, being rejected out of consideration. She pondered that for a while, and then she decided Brian knew a bit too much about women, whereas she knew disgracefully little about men.

She turned toward him restlessly, slipping an arm around his waist and nestling her cheek in his shoulder. His chest was bare, his hair furry-soft on her smooth flesh above the nightgown. He wore pajama bottoms—in honor of that rest he said she needed? She slid a knee between his and relaxed, closing her eyes. The fit was perfect.

"Leigh."

"Mmmm." She curled closer yet to the sudden change in his heartbeat, to the swell of hardness pressing against her stomach. He shifted. Gradually, she shifted with him, the feeling of being close to him inducing a lazy somnolence that was pleasing all in itself. Somewhat.

"Red."

"Mmmm."

His palm suddenly stroked up her arm to the hollow of her collarbone, and then his fingers splayed in the thickness of her hair with far too much tension for a man who was nearly asleep. "You've had much too little rest the last few days," he whispered roughly.

"True," she whispered back obediently. "But I can't seem to sleep just yet. Would you rather I moved to the other bed, Brian?"

He did not want her to move away. His body tensed in total rejection of that idea. He knew so much, her arrogant lover: how to break impregnable shells, how to bridge the strongest defenses . . . yet not enough, not that night, to turn down a lady who wanted to love him. And this time it wasn't *being* loved that was on her mind, but learning to return the loving sensations he had brought to her.

Her hands glided over muscle and bone, sinew and flesh. Her lips trailed, a little shyer, uncertain of his response. She was not a femme fatale and had no weapons against the kind of sexually experienced women he played with. She had only love. And yet he suddenly gave in, bending over her with restless, drugging kisses. It thrilled her to know that her hands had the power to make him lose that endless control of his.

She could not seem to stop touching him. The feel of

his hair, the way the flesh of his shoulders became pliant in her hands, the way his body took on heat when she reached between his thighs. And the way he looked at her when he surged over her, that instant before she knew he was going to take her . . . her arms raised, drawing him down to her, drawing him into that moist, silky darkness. It was Leigh's nature to give and to reach out in loving; and now she could love totally, with no shadows of the past intruding.

Chapter 15

ON THE SURFACE the cocktail party for Brian's clients went very well. Leigh had made the drinks and canapés ahead of time and the condominium was spotless. She'd felt a surge of ambition right from the beginning, a need to have the meeting go well for Brian and a hope that she would have the chance to soothe a few troubled waters: Brian made no secret of not liking the Harrises. In fact, even before they got there, he'd made it clear that they could take his design or leave it; he had done all the compromising he intended to do. Feeling ultra-feminine in a water-colored dress that swirled to her knees and showed off her tan, Leigh knew the project meant more to him than he let on and acted accordingly.

Phil Harris was around sixty and a perfect stand-in for Colonel Sanders; Leigh wished she could weather his heavy-handed humor with a bourbon—or four—but because of her pregnancy, she could only sip her ginger ale and smile. His wife, Irene, dressed fussily in lavender, was a nonstop talker. The business manager of the group was John Blake, a short man with small cat's eyes that seemed to miss very little of what went on around him. He refused food or drink or any other kind of entertainment; he had his mind strictly on business until Leigh finally ferreted out an interest in fishing. She was able to raise no smiles, but still felt a modicum of success when she at least got him to sit down and stop his restless roving while waiting for the others to get down to brass tacks.

Phil's son, Dan Harris, was as tall as Brian and as thin as a sapling, with light hair and colorless eyes. He had as much interest in business as a cat in swimming; he cared only for the profits in this deal, and was eager to talk money. Rita, Dan's wife, was a dark-haired beauty in a red peasant-styled dress. Leigh felt an instant antipathy toward her when she positioned herself on the arm of Brian's chair, leaning over, talking and laughing intimately with him. No one else seemed to notice, or perhaps they were used to her, or perhaps they just didn't care. But Leigh cared: Rita's behavior, and the way Brian seemed to lap it up, reminded her forcefully of how tenuous a hold she had on her husband.

After the better part of an hour, Phil finally brought up business and the glasses were set down. A few details were argued, and then Brian's proposal was accepted. A basic contract was set before him, to be returned in the morning after he'd looked it over. Finally the Harrises and John White rose as a group to leave. When the door was closed behind them, Leigh gave an audible sigh of relief. The next time Brian described people as being "difficult," she would be more inclined to believe him. But it was all over now: He had his project, and Leigh felt a certain pride in having been part of that.

Brian, however, did not appear to be in a mood for rejoicing. With a fresh drink in his hand, he had opened the sliding doors to the balcony and was staring out over the ocean. Leigh started gathering the glasses and dishes to clean up, and as quietly as possible removed herself to the kitchen. It was obvious from the intent concentration on Brian's face that he wanted no company. She had seen the beginnings of a "brood" coming on before. Without disturbing him, she snatched up a sweater and went out the back door for a few minutes of fresh air.

The sunset had just finished its color splash; the stars were barely visible and a faint hue of violent was still reflected on the horizon. Leigh reclined on a chaise longue on the small patio, feeling peace flood over her like a warm blanket.

Brian's footsteps startled her some minutes later. She got up instantly with a smile of welcome, but the smile faded as she saw the tension in his face.

"You heard me tell the Harrises the project will take closer to four months than two," he began abruptly.

"I heard you, Brian," she answered quietly. "But so what? Not knowing how long we'd be away, I didn't take on any new clients before we left. And you arranged things with your partners, so what's the problem?"

"No problem at all," he said tersely. "But surely you don't think I'd let you stay here, away from your own doctor, and especially now that I know about the possibility of twins?"

"I don't understand what all the fuss is about," she told him. "Surely I can take a plane up once a month to see Dr. Franklin and—"

"My schedule will be crazy. I won't have much time for you. You know how I am when I'm working on something big, Leigh."

"Yes, I do know. And I understand. Brian, I love you—"

"You think you do," he cut her off sharply. "Look, Leigh, I need some time to myself. I'm going for a walk." And with that, he turned abruptly on his heel and left.

He was gone a long time. Leigh stayed outside until she was shivering in the damp cool air, shivering in apprehension as well. Why didn't he want her to stay? Could it be that he was planning an affair with Rita Harris, and the presence of his wife—his pregnant wife—would cramp his style? Despair touched her heart.

An hour passed and then two, and finally she gave in to weariness, going inside to wash and undress for bed, listening intently for the sound of the door. The lights were off and she was under the covers when he finally came in.

"You're going home, Leigh," he told her flatly. It was a tone he had used before, one that brooked no discussion.

"Why?" She switched on the light by the bed, making no pretense of being any nearer sleep than she was. "What are you talking about?" She didn't dare mention Rita, show herself as a jealous, shrewish wife. He had married her precisely because he'd thought he could do so and still retain his freedom.

He stripped off his tie, shirt, and then the rest of his clothes. "Leigh, I'm going to be very busy for the next few months. I won't be there for you if you need me. At home you've at least got Robert around during the day if you don't feel well, and you're only a phone call away from your doctor."

"Brian, Robert could come down here and stay," she said reasonably. "We have room. It would do him good."

He didn't bother to look at her as he switched out the light and climbed into the other side of the bed. "I'll book you a flight at the end of the week."

"You can book a dozen flights if you want," Leigh snapped.

Brian was silent for a long time. And then suddenly he switched on the light and turned to her. Leigh had her arms folded rigidly under her breasts and her eyes were ablaze with fury and unshed tears.

"It won't work, Red. Not for me," he said coldly. "Do I have to come right out and say I don't want you here?"

She lowered her eyes so that he wouldn't see the pain in them, and immediately turned away, lying on her side. The hurt nearly choked her. "I'll book my own flight in the morning," she said hoarsely.

He turned out the light again, and as if in a bad dream she felt his palm on the back of her neck, pretending to soothe with incredible gentleness. She jabbed back with her elbow; hit out at his hand. "You have to be joking, Brian! Leave me alone!" It was hard enough being told he didn't want her, without revealing to him just how vulnerable she was where he was concerned. There wasn't a chance in hell she would ever stay where she wasn't wanted.

He drew her protesting furiously to the cradle of his chest.

A trickle of wetness slid down her cheeks, and she lodged her hands helplessly between the two of them. "I hate you!" she hissed.

"That's just the problem, Leigh, you don't," he said gently. "Do you think I don't know what you're feeling? You're so sure you're in love with me, Red." He gave her a penny of distance, and she reached up hurriedly to wipe away the tears on her cheeks. "It's not love, Leigh. It's only the feeling a woman has for the first man who's made love to her. You'll be fine once you get away from me; there hasn't been too much time together . . . like this. You're just in a hurry to love, now that you know what it's about, and it shows in your every action. You're going to get hurt if you stay here. A breather will do us both some good, and then we'll see."

She didn't argue. She knew from the tone in his voice that there wasn't any point. The threat of tears passed. She had never realized how much pride she had—until now, when it seemed to be the only thing she had. She sat up stiffly on the edge of the bed. "What I felt for you, Brian," she said quietly, "was alive a long time before you made love to me."

"Leigh," he said gently.

She stood up to avoid the touch of his arm. "No," she said firmly.

"You fought hard to have that child in you conceived," he said harshly. "One of us has to think of what's best for—"

"Oh, shut up, Brian!" Leigh stormed. If nothing else, she hoped to part from him with honesty. It was for his sake and not hers that she was leaving. She thought the less of him for not admitting it, when all of the humiliation was on her side. "I'll take care of myself from now on, and the baby, too. I don't want any more help from you of any kind! What's 'best for me' no longer has anything to do with you!"

Leigh left before sunrise, being careful not to awaken Brian. She took only her purse and a small tote bag of belongings she always carried with her. There were no frequently scheduled flights from the Keys, so she knew she couldn't count on getting a seat, particularly at this time of year. She ended up renting a car to Miami, because she had no choice.

By dinnertime she was back home in Chicago exhausted, hollow-eyed, and thoroughly miserable after having been sick throughout most of the flight. She could hear Monster barking and Robert scolding the pup even before the door was opened. Outside, snow was still lush on the ground, although a thaw was forecast for the following week.

As soon as the door opened, Leigh threw her arms around Robert and burst into tears. "What on earth? Oh, honey," Robert said, his voice familiarly soothing. His shock at seeing her—and alone—was clear, but being Robert he didn't express anything but the comfort she so obviously needed. She was fed soup and crackers, regaled with a list of achievements Monster had failed to master, and assured that she had been sorely missed.

"Got eighteen inches of snow one day." The blizzard had shut down the city, and as Robert told Leigh the details he studied her every feature.

As she did his. Robert was so dear to her, and he didn't look well. She had been gone less than two weeks; how could he have aged so rapidly? "Have you been feeling all right?" she asked sharply.

"God, you're starting in already," he groaned.

The kitchen table had never looked so good, with Robert's wrinkled face on the other side of it. The silky black pup was nestled on the tips of Leigh's shoes, fast asleep. The kitchen was and always had been her favorite room in the house, and even the memories of Brian here were pleasant ones. But Brian didn't want her—she mustn't think of him.

"So," Robert said carefully, "I gather we're not to mention his name or talk about it?"

At times, Leigh thought sadly, Robert could be heartbreakingly sensitive. "I love you, Robert," she said. "If I haven't told you before—"

"You'll give me indigestion," he interrupted gruffly.

She smiled, or tried to. "I want to move, and sell this house. Do you think you're up for it?"

"Why?" he demanded.

"Because . . ." Because she'd just had twelve hours in which to think of something else besides Brian. "I don't know. There's to be a new baby, and I don't like the idea of crowding it with old memories. I've been happy enough here, for most of the time, but . . . my mother wasn't. And David—certainly wasn't a happy man."

"A fresh start for the baby, is that it?"

She nodded, and poured herself a second cup of tea.

"You have a place in mind?"

"In a way."

"Someplace that's for sale?"

"I haven't the least idea," Leigh said frankly. "For a long time, there's been a certain house I liked, Robert. I just thought I'd knock on the door tomorrow and ask—"

"You're not serious, honey. You can't do that."

"Of course I can, Robert. I can do whatever I have to do to survive."

Survival was the issue, for more than four months. Long ago, Leigh had determined what made a life worth waking up to: someone to care for, someone to love. She had Robert already, and soon she would have the baby, and never mind that the bleakness in her heart seemed to overshadow everything.

She survived the move and sale of the old place during her sixth month of pregnancy. By some miracle, the woman who lived in the new house had been debating moving closer to her relatives in the South and Leigh's offer settled the issue. The house was Brian's design, and Leigh had sought it out deliberately—not to continually torture herself with reminders of the past, but as a legacy for her child. The house was as perfect as she knew it would be, all space and serenity; and the use of glass and wood and earth textures seemed to bring the outside in. Her face grew gaunt as she worked feverishly with endless piles of boxes to pack and unpack, yards and yards of curtains to put up, and the baby's room to decorate.

She survived Robert's increasing frailty. He liked the house well enough because it was all on one floor, but each day it seemed harder for him to get around despite all of Leigh's efforts to protect him. He'd taken the move in his stride, but the doctor's confirmation that Leigh indeed was carrying twins had upset him greatly. "Leigh, you can't handle it," he cautioned her. "One will like nights and the other days; one will sleep while the other's up . . ." She tried to console him by joking that at least it was not triplets, but his feeble smile didn't hide the increasing lines of fatigue and worry on his face.

And she survived the phone calls and the mail. She had answered the phone that first time, the night of her home-coming, to hear Brian demanding to know why she had stolen from his side in the middle of the night.

"I would have driven you to the airport," he said angrily. "For heaven's sake, Leigh, what's the matter with you?"

"Nothing," she said frostily. "I'm perfectly fine, Brian. It's just, well, I've had time to think. I've decided you're right, we need a breather from each other. I see that I was mistaken after all. It was sex, not love, and I . . . well, I just can't deal with it all right now. I have a million things to do in the next few months to prepare for the baby. I have to get a nursery ready: buy the crib, the layette, a playpen. Robert isn't too well, either. He needs me. And you're busy, too. When you come back to Chicago, we'll talk."

"I see," he said curtly. "The old self-sufficient Leigh, eh? But don't forget, it's my baby, too. And I'm concerned about Robert. I . . . Oh, hell, I'm late for a dinner with the Harrises, but I'll call you tomorrow, okay? And I'll write."

So, he wanted to keep up a connection—for the baby's sake—and he cared about Robert, too. Good, let him talk to Robert then, between his dinners with Rita Harris. From that moment on, Leigh made herself unavailable to Brian. She threw away his letters, unopened. She told Robert to take his calls and say that she wasn't in. "Don't question me, Robert," she pleaded. "It's all over between Brian and me. I don't want to discuss it."

Even with the move and her deliberately unlisted phone number, Brian tracked her down somehow and called Robert regularly, at specific times that she guessed were prear-ranged. "I told you she had help for the moving . . . Why don't you two settle this thing, anyway . . . If you care so damned much . . . The doctor isn't sure . . ." Although Leigh couldn't help overhearing snippets of conversation, she and Robert pretended the phone calls didn't happen, and they never discussed the mail.

She survived spring in the new house, knowing Brian had directed the landscaping for it. She could not doubt it. The dogwood, crab apple, and two plum trees blossomed, their heady scents permeating the grounds. The maples, careless about adding their leaves in the spring, finally succumbed to a steady stream of warm days, and whispering breezes shivered through the fresh green leaves. There was the scent of jonquils and hyacinths and of freshly mowed grass, and violets carpeted the floor of the woods to the back of the house. The landscape was designed for spring and for lovers, for memories not yet made and those that never would be.

The nights were the hardest to survive. She dreamed of Brian, over and over again. She dreamed of that Christmas in Minnesota, when Monster was a pup and Brian was so solicitous. She threw her arms around her dream lover, and he held her, just held her, for an eternity. Time swirled and they were on the museum steps, the waves of Lake Michigan catching the late afternoon sun. He kissed her and kept on kissing her, and she felt herself slowly descending into the cool silk waters of a pool on a day so hot . . . so hot. And making love the first time: the power, the velvet power of his hands! She would have staked her life that there was no such response in her, that her fear was unbridgeable, that she could never again bear being helpless at the hands of any man. But she *had* been helpless, and there had been no fear, no degradation. She had felt revered, loved, cherished when he made love to her. Yet it hadn't meant a thing to him.

She always woke from the dreams with tears in her eyes. For those moments in the darkness, she hated the burden she carried. If she hadn't been like this—big and burdensome and clumsily unattractive—she might possibly, just possibly, have risked all her pride and sanity on one last try to be with him. "I don't want you," he had said, and the endless refrain echoed over and over as she feverishly tried to keep busy. So how could he possibly want her as she was? Especially when he could have Rita, and any other woman he desired. Night after night, she told herself that this *had* to pass; she *had* to start living again.

Chapter 16

LEIGH WAS SO accustomed to waking at the first light of dawn that the morning of June 7th seemed no different. Perhaps a little different, she thought wearily, as she stretched and snuggled tiredly against the pillow.

She'd seen Dr. Franklin the day before. In her usual nononsense manner, the obstetrician had told Leigh that she wanted to induce labor on the 15th—two weeks early. She didn't want to let the twins take on too much weight in their crowded space. Reassuringly, Dr. Franklin had told Leigh that both babies had strong heartbeats . . . and then delivered the lecture Leigh had heard before: the one about the shadows under her eyes, about her being the only patient the doctor had to encourage to eat more.

Drowsily, Leigh noted now that it was raining outside, a gentle patter against the French doors that led to the patio outside her bedroom. The sound was lulling, hypnotic, and she found herself falling asleep again. At nine she startled awake, feeling more refreshed than she had in weeks. As quickly as she could, she washed and dressed, then ambled into the kitchen. "Robert?" She was almost smiling, anticipating his reaction to her oversleeping. He had been scolding her for weeks about her early risings, but she knew he would now have a comment like, "I see you *finally* got around to getting up?" or "It's so late it's nearly time to go back to bed!"

The kitchen, curiously, was empty. No fresh coffee, no breakfast dishes soaking, no paper, no crossword puzzle on the table.

Her smile faded. "Robert?" She opened the back door that led onto a cement patio. The smells of the morning rain were fresh and strong; the wrought-iron furniture still glistened with raindrops like crystals in the emerging sun. She closed the door.

"Robert?"

She peered into the library and opened the front door that faced the drive. From the distance, she could see the morning newspaper still in its yellow box and undoubtedly damp at the edges. Robert was nowhere to be seen.

Instinctively, her arms folded protectively around her stomach. She closed the front door and walked down the hall to Robert's room. She knocked on the closed door, and received no answer.

"Robert?"

It was just as if he were asleep. His eyes were closed; he was lying on his back with one arm extended neatly over the covers. His face looked almost smooth again, with a far gentler expression than the one he usually wore.

Leigh sank down on the edge of the bed. She knew it had been coming for a long time; she had even prayed that it might end just this way, that there would be no pain. Still... "Oh, my friend," she whispered softly. The sadness flowed over her in long, endless waves. This was Robert, a mixture of father and mother and friend, in a way no one else could ever duplicate. He had loved and protected her with a devotion that she had never understood, one she had always felt guilty about. She had loved him, yes, had seen that he was secure and cared for as best she could, but she had always felt that he did far more for her than she for him. He had been her anchor, her ballast.

The tears fell soundlessly, and Leigh rocked back and forth, her arms folded around her swelling stomach, allowing her grief its expression and her sorrow its freedom.

On the day before the funeral, she wired Brian because she could not face a phone call. The message was simple and short, and overtly it asked for nothing. Just, "Brian, Robert died," and the time and place of the funeral. She knew she owed him the notification, knew his fondness for the older man had been genuine. Yet she hoped all the same that he wouldn't come.

Leigh did not think she could deal with any more emotion. The last few days had been bearable; she hadn't had time to think but could only react as each problem came up. Dinner to be made; Monster to be walked; clothes to be washed; endless callers to entertain and all of the arrangements: Each was a problem she seemed to grope with blindly, as if the whole world was suddenly terrifyingly unfamiliar and frightening.

The nights had been much worse, filled with endless hours of despair and weariness. There was suddenly no feeling for the twins inside of her, no reason to get up in the morning. She could not cope; she had lost her best and only friend. Thinking herself independent and in control, she had never realized how much she relied on the old family retainer who had been so dear to her to see her through each day. Especially since she'd lost Brian. She had thought to leave him before he left her, but she hadn't been able to cut him out of her heart. She had assumed time would ease the pain of that loss, but it hadn't, and with the fresh loss of Robert, she found herself missing Brian more than ever. And over these past months, just the knowledge that Robert was in communication with Brian, even though she herself wasn't, had been a strange comfort. Now all links were broken and she felt herself totally alone.

And so she waited through the long day of the funeral, feeling ever more certain that Brian wouldn't come. She ought to feel relieved—she'd feared seeing him again— and yet, she was consumed with a sense of desolation.

Her attorney, Mr. Adams, drove her to the funeral and delivered the short and personal eulogy. Leigh refused to

listen. There was nothing real about the box that was put
in the ground—it had no relationship at all to the man she
had known—and in a strangely detached way she resented
the whole ceremony. She had few memories of Robert that
were not good ones, and there was no question of putting
them to rest, nor did she want to.

Mr. Adams drove her home in the middle of the afternoon, and then rather awkwardly invited himself in. He then
proceeded to sit determinedly in a chair in the living room,
talking monotonously of her father and events in the past
when he had known Robert, when she was just a child.
Leigh felt so weary and confused that she hardly recognized
what he was doing; it was only as dinnertime approached
and the white-haired attorney cleared his throat and offered
to stay the night that she realized what was going on. Mr.
Adams was doing his best to be kind; he was concerned
about her being alone in this time of mourning.

"There's absolutely no need," she assured him. She
wanted, in fact, to be by herself. "Mr. Adams, you've been
wonderful to me over the last few days. I'm sorry I haven't
seemed more appreciative."

"Didn't expect you to be," he said rather stiffly, and then
paused. "I tried to contact Mr. Hathaway, Leigh. I called
Florida, and I tried his office here in Chicago."

"You shouldn't have done that," she said sharply. "You
know I asked you—"

"Yes," the attorney agreed. "I know." Absently, he rubbed
his forehead. "I'm afraid under the circumstances I found
it difficult to think only as your legal adviser, Leigh. At
any rate, I couldn't get hold of your husband. That's one
of the reasons I offered to stay."

Leigh apologized to Mr. Adams for her sharpness, but
assured him that she could manage very well on her own.
She ushered him out, and when the sound of his car engine
finally faded down the drive, she simply leaned against the
door for a long moment. The house was totally silent except
for the ticking of a clock in the dining room. She had been
waiting for this moment. She hadn't been aware of it before,
yet now she knew that she had been anticipating it and
wondering exactly how the silence was going to affect her.

It was past five, and she had no more reason to hope or

fear that anyone else was coming. Mindlessly, she heated some soup on the stove, fed the puppy, cleared away the clutter. She let Monster out, unloosed and brushed her hair, kicked off her shoes, but did not seem to have quite enough energy to get undressed yet. She let the puppy back in and closed the curtains against the late afternoon sun. Mechanical movements all of them, to block out that sound of silence. And suddenly there was nothing more to be done, and even Monster refused to create any further distractions, falling into an exhausted heap beneath a chair. Her condition conspired against her; her back hurt and she just had no energy left to invent tasks that would put off the quiet any longer.

She sat, finally, on the edge of the couch in the living room, and became part of the stillness. The shadows of daylight lengthened, blurred, and finally faded with the sunset. Even the babies seemed asleep inside of her.

The rap on the door was so unexpected that she started at the sound of it. She momentarily debated the possibility of simply ignoring the visitor, but the knocking was persistent. Awkwardly, she got to her feet and ambled to the door.

Brian had a large brown sack in his hand. His light gray suit had an unaccustomed rumpled look to it, and his tie was improperly knotted. There were tired lines around his eyes, and his hair was disheveled, as if the wind had had its way with it.

Leigh's detachment of the last few hours had been so complete that for a moment she could only stare disbelievingly at him. And suddenly she regretted, terribly, sending him that telegram, because the first look of him immediately stirred her emotions, and she absolutely could not take any more pain, not now.

He looked back at her with an inscrutable gaze, and yet she thought she caught a glimpse of anguish, a pain that reflected her own, in his eyes before he brought the shutter down on them. His jaw tightened, and then just as quickly relaxed.

"Let me in, Red. I've got enough Chinese food in here for an army."

It was Brian who switched on the lights, closed the door,

led Leigh into the kitchen, and searched through cupboards and drawers for dishes and utensils. He simply took over, in a manner she had almost forgotten. She could not seem to stop looking at him, but she could not say anything, either. He was thinner; gaunt planes stood out on his face, but his expression was as unfathomable as ever. She could not tell if he was glad to see her or sorry, if he had come out of a sense of duty or something more. In her mind and dreams these past months she had envisioned a thousand times over what she would say and do if she saw him again, but she had never imagined that she would be too tired and heartworn to even think, or that her stomach would be so full and cumbersome, or that she would be so thoroughly unable to hide her feelings of vulnerability and wariness. She was always perfectly dressed in her dreams, slim and chic, with exactly the right words at the tip of her tongue and a nonchalance that was devastating.

Now she found herself seated across the table from him, the food on her plate untouched. With both a smile and an impatient sigh, he wedged his chair closer to hers, filling her fork with food and bringing it to her lips.

"Brian," she protested. The rest of her response was stilled as the fork was not too gently shoved in. She snatched it away with a rueful glance at him. "I just made soup a little while ago."

"I saw. It's still on the stove. You never turned it on."

So she ate, while he told her about the house she was living in, how he had come to design it, one of his first. "The kitchen gave me fits. At this point, as you already know, I'm an expert at rubbery eggs; but at the time I couldn't boil water, so I had no idea of how to design a livable floor plan." He smiled at her, a totally natural smile that she found herself returning.

When the dinner was over, she rose, awkwardly of course, her face averted so she wouldn't have to see his reaction to her burgeoning figure. Brian got up at the same time and helped her clear the dishes. His hands brushed against her arms, moving her aside or reaching around her—sheerly accidental movements, and yet they sent her pulses racing uncomfortably. How *could* it be . . . the stirrings of desire, the craving to be held in his arms? It was like a physical pain, blotting out everything, even Robert.

"Leigh?"

She turned to him, feeling her heart race as she saw him searching her face as intently as she was searching his, drinking in the sight of her, the exact color of her hair, every plane and hollow of her face. Slowly he moved closer, and then she was cradled so tightly she could not breathe, and her heart was beating against his. She buried her face in his shirt.

"I couldn't come sooner," he murmured. "I didn't know. I was on the project site when Western Union first called the condo. They were trying again when I got home, and then I had trouble getting a flight. I called, but there was no answer."

"I love you, Brian."

He tensed just a little and drew back, but his eyes never left her face.

"I didn't want to ask for your help," she continued painfully. "I hated it, knowing you'd come out of a sense of responsibility—I never wanted to be a responsibility to you. But when Robert died—"

"Oh, Leigh . . ."

"I hoped you wouldn't come, but now that you're here I have to know. You have to tell me, Brian," she burst out passionately. "Why? Was it because we were so different you didn't even want to try? Because I was so inexperienced, so inhibited? Or so unglamorous, compared to the other women? Was it Rita Harris? Was it because I like to cook? Are my eyes the wrong color?"

"Your eyes," he said gravely, "are the perfect color, Leigh. They always were." His fingers curled in her hair, burying themselves in that copper thickness. "You're the sexiest lady I know, Red. And thank God you like to cook; we certainly couldn't live on my rubbery eggs. As for Rita Harris—oh Lord, did you think . . . ? I haven't seen her since the last time I saw you, love. You're it, Leigh. There's been no other woman, I swear. I want no other woman." She looked up at him with the shimmer of tears in her eyes. "I love you, Leigh."

She had never heard that wrenching, painful tone in his voice before.

"But you sent me away, Brian. And all these months . . ."

"I had to, Leigh. Can't you understand? We didn't form this peculiar alliance of ours out of love. You'd never even gotten your feet wet in love before, and it's so easy to mistake the first throes of passion for the real thing. That's what I thought you were doing, and I had to make you leave before you broke your heart over someone you really didn't love—me. I never meant to touch you, Red, but then I couldn't stop myself. I wanted to be the one to show you love and how good it could be for you."

"And you did," Leigh said softly.

Tenderly, he kissed her. Then he drew back swiftly, his eyes boring into hers with a need so intense she wanted to cry. "But once wasn't enough, not for me—I wanted to be the one *all* the time. But I'd rushed you, Leigh, stormed your defenses. Don't you see, Red? It would have been taking advantage.

Almost without being aware of it, Leigh was cradled in the nook of his shoulder and led out of the kitchen, past the living room, and down the narrow passage of hall. "If I'd just understood how you felt, Brian. I thought you wanted Rita, wanted to go back to your playboy lifestyle. I loved you before we ever made love. I tried to tell you. I've loved you so long."

Before she could protest, he had the zipper down on her white linen dress, the lamp on by her bed, and the two of them were leaning back against the pillows. The slip did little to cover the shape of her figure, and he gazed at it tenderly, stroking the silky fabric that covered her abdomen. The weight of the babies nestled between them, as she relaxed for the first time in days. The lower-back pain she had felt all day was forgotten; and her self-consciousness over her appearance . . . well, it just wasn't there anymore. He touched her with love, one arm folded around her and the other resting on her burden.

"I thought I would go out of my mind all these months, thinking you didn't want me." His mouth twisted in a small, unwilling smile. "No, I didn't want to love you in the beginning. I had a few barriers of my own to break down.

For a man who didn't want ties, Red, I kept finding myself in an incredible hurry to finish work so I could come home to dinner. I expected demands, Red, but you didn't make any. You so obviously were amazed at even the least consideration. I expected to be bored, but you've got so many interests, Leigh, that I can barely keep up with you. And I expected at least a basic exchange of needs, but while you were all prepared to take on mine, it wasn't the same the other way, now was it? That evening when you barely had the strength to hold your head over a basin . . . I could have killed you, Leigh, for not coming to me."

He shifted, still gazing at her as he brought her pillow down and encouraged her to lie flat. He pulled the covers up protectively to her chin and lay on his side next to her. Leigh watched his every move, filled with love, savoring each word. "And then there was this," he admitted, as his left hand again caressed the mound of her stomach. "I've been jealous from the beginning, Leigh. You so obviously intended to put the baby first, before anything else in your life. And even after I made love to you, I still thought it would be that way. I could just picture a houseful of children where all I would ever have of you was the leftovers." He paused. "I was raised in a home with four boys, all closely spaced together. I hated the confusion, the lack of privacy. You couldn't even read a book in my house, or study, or concentrate on anything. And then my dad died, and I was responsible for the lot of them."

"So you don't want your children raised that way," Leigh said calmly. "I don't either, Brian. I love children, but they're only a short-term loan; they grow up and leave, and that's as it should be. I never wanted a dozen, or a houseful. Just one. And when you first met me, Brian, that's all I thought I would ever have. A husband should be forever, but for me there was no forever . . ."

His hand on her stomach raised up noticeably. "Good God, what's that?"

"They're just turning over, Brian."

His hand remained until the motion stopped; and then, with a very set expression on his face, he kissed her firmly and got up. "Time to erase those circles under your eyes, Leigh."

He would listen to no protests. There were a thousand things she wanted to say to him, but their love was so fragile, the admission of it so new.

"You think I want to leave you, Red?" he reproached her. "You're out of your mind! But for tonight and tonight only, you'll sleep alone. Oh, yes, Leigh, you need some solid, uninterrupted rest. No!" He ignored her gesture of protest. "I'll be right in the next room. Just call me if you need anything."

Chapter 17

"BRIAN!" It was more a scream than a call. The pain came again, searing sharp, lasting endless seconds before it finally passed.

Brian appeared in shorts and bare feet, his brows knitted together and his black eyes alert. The night-light beside her bed was already on and he blinked as his eyes adjusted to the brightness.

"It's not going the way it's supposed to, Brian. I can't breathe like Dr. Franklin said. It was all right in the beginning, but—"

"How long?" he interrupted sharply.

"Since about one." Another pain started, bringing beads of perspiration to her forehead as she fought to bear with the wave while it peaked and finally receded.

"Since *one*—you damned idiot! It's five o'clock! Why the hell didn't you call me?"

"They were only coming every fifteen or twenty minutes. But then it changed so quickly."

Furiously, he fumbled at the notepad she pointed to next to the bed, snapping questions at her as he telephoned the doctor's answering service. Dr. Franklin would be calling in shortly. He had barely hung up the phone when the doctor called back, and Brian explained to her that Leigh had gone into labor. Dr. Franklin said she'd be right over.

"I'm glad she is coming here," Leigh said. "I didn't want to lie in some hospital room for hours."

"Where you're going to lie is directly across my knee when this is over, lady! Those happen to be my kids in there, you know." He left her, on the run, grabbing his shirt and pants en route to the kitchen, where he put a pan on the stove. The sound of drawers being slammed could be heard all the way in the bedroom. And then his face reappeared in the doorway. "Where the hell are the linens?"

"What are you doing?"

"What I *did,* thank God, is some research with my brother Richard. Towels, Leigh?" he repeated impatiently.

She could not tell him at that very instant. When she could, there were tears in her eyes from the exertion, and she was digging her nails into Brian's wrists. She had been prepared for the dull, aching cramps; they were short and well spaced and she had been practicing the breathing exercises for months. But she was so very tired now, and there had been so much trauma in the last few days. As each pain grew in strength and intensity, so did the feeling of panic . . . until she cried out to Brian, and saw him, and felt the strength in his hands. For one strange moment, she even imagined she saw tears in his eyes. "I can't stand to see you hurting, Leigh."

"It's all right," she said softly. But she did not have to be told she was not going to make it to the hospital. And then Dr. Franklin arrived, and she knew she wanted Brian to stay for the delivery.

"Leigh, listen, sweetheart," he said soothingly. "I'll be right here. It's all right. Dr. Franklin will take good care of you."

She was close, very close. Her body told her to push, to work—and it was work, more than pain. And she knew she wanted her husband to work with her, to aid her in the effort to bring their offspring into the world. It was partly a cry from her heart, perhaps not totally rational either, a cry for Brian to bond with his children—*his* children. And it was partly the most basic statement of love and trust.

"Red, damn it, push!"

She smiled at his frantic tone, never believing that she would have the occasion to calm *him*. But she was wrong. She had exactly enough time to murmur, "Help me, Brian. Our children are being born. Help me."

It all happened very quickly after that. The first was a red-faced, dark-haired, skinny, squally girl. Leigh would never forget the wonder, the shock on Brian's face when he took the baby from her. The second was also a girl— they were identical twins. Red and wrinkled as the babies were, Leigh thought them the most beautiful creatures on earth. And she knew Brian felt the same.

"Never again though, Leigh," he said. "Next time you go to the hospital *months* ahead of time. Do you hear me? I'm going to lock you in there with a whole team of doctors."

"Yes, Brian." Next time? Her heart soared.

He kissed her, long and lingeringly, before she was strapped on a stretcher with the infants to be taken to the hospital. "I'd rather stay with you," she whispered to Brian. "It's over, and lots of women have their children at home these days. I don't see why I have to—"

"You can have your way for the next thousand years, Red, I promise you, but not tonight," he scolded sternly.

"That'll teach you to sleep in a separate room," she whispered. She was thoroughly exhausted, and yet the smile on her face was immovable, a fixture of happiness.

Brian's smile was no less real, and she swore she heard him laughing as the doors were closed on the ambulance and it pulled out of the drive.

The whisper of a breeze from the open doorway brought the scent of roses into the bedroom. It was nearing midnight; and the house was quiet and peaceful. The moonlight etched silver on the bare back of the man beside her.

Leigh fought the sleep that threatened, wanting to savor the silence and sensations of the warm night. Loretta and Kim were almost six weeks old now, and no longer the red-faced squirming bundles they had been at birth. They now looked very much like their father, dark-haired and dark-eyed, but with Leigh's creamy skin. Although the twins were identical in appearance, each had her own distinct personality. Kim was a peaceful baby, her eyes taking in the wonder of the world with every passing day. Loretta was more apt to be more restless, less content; she would be constantly carried, night and day, if she could get away with it. Which she could, when Brian was around. For one who was wary of "squalling brats," Brian had done an abrupt about-face that still caused Leigh to smile.

Ruth had offered to come for the first month, but Brian suggested she come a little later. Instead, he had hired a night nurse, and had taken three weeks off from work to help Leigh himself. On the evenings he was forced to bring work home, he carted at least one of the twins into the library with him. They never fussed for him. They either slept or gurgled contentedly in their infant seats, next to his drawing board or on the couch, intrigued by the sound of a pencil scratch or the crackle of paper.

Leigh sighed, unable to believe how absolutely happy she was. She heard the sound of a baby's cry, and instinctively she stilled. Brian also was all attention, so she knew he wasn't asleep. "Loretta," he said perceptively.

They both listened to the soothing sounds of the night nurse, the cries abruptly ceasing as the infant was cared for.

"We won't need her much longer," Leigh said of the nurse. Kim was already sleeping through the night, and it seemed foolish to have outside help for only an occasional night feeding. In the beginning, Leigh had been desperate for rest, but now she was feeling perfectly fit again, with as much energy as she had ever had.

"We'll see," Brian murmured. "I don't want you all tired out, Leigh."

"Are you awake?" she whispered a few minutes later.

He chuckled. "Getting there," he said dryly.

"Good." She kissed the back of his neck, and then rained soft kisses down the cool skin of his spine. With her fingertips, she erased them, in smooth, soothing caresses, and then started all over again. "I've been looking at that back of yours for nearly over a month," she complained.

He turned, pressing her back into the sheets, and drew

her hands together in one of his own. "You haven't been back to the doctor yet, Red," he reminded her.

His chest was more interesting than his back. Her fingers traced patterns in the swirls of hair, followed by her lips, soft and curious. "I won't tell if you won't," she whispered. Crouched on her knees in the darkness, she put both arms on the sides of his face so that she could lean over and gently kiss his neck and ears and forehead. She drew back to look at him, love and a question in her eyes. "I think this is called a very amateur seduction. I love you, Brian. I feel like singing it from the rooftops."

With one smooth, sure move, their positions were reversed, and Leigh was pressed into the sheets with Brian staring down at her. She could feel his love, a tangible essence between them, and she could feel her whole body react to it, trembling in anticipation. And then his lips came down on hers, and the trembling ceased.

_____ 06872-1 **SPRING FEVER #108** Simone Hadary
_____ 06873-X **IN THE ARMS OF A STRANGER #109** Deborah Joyce
_____ 06874-8 **TAKEN BY STORM #110** Kay Robbins
_____ 06899-3 **THE ARDENT PROTECTOR #111** Amanda Kent
_____ 07200-1 **A LASTING TREASURE #112** Cally Hughes $1.95
_____ 07203-6 **COME WINTER'S END #115** Claire Evans $1.95
_____ 07212-5 **SONG FOR A LIFETIME #124** Mary Haskell $1.95
_____ 07213-3 **HIDDEN DREAMS #125** Johanna Phillips $1.95
_____ 07214-1 **LONGING UNVEILED #126** Meredith Kingston $1.95
_____ 07215-X **JADE TIDE #127** Jena Hunt $1.95
_____ 07216-8 **THE MARRYING KIND #128** Jocelyn Day $1.95
_____ 07217-6 **CONQUERING EMBRACE #129** Ariel Tierney $1.95
_____ 07218-4 **ELUSIVE DAWN #130** Kay Robbins $1.95
_____ 07219-2 **ON WINGS OF PASSION #131** Beth Brookes $1.95
_____ 07220-6 **WITH NO REGRETS #132** Nuria Wood $1.95
_____ 07221-4 **CHERISHED MOMENTS #133** Sarah Ashley $1.95
_____ 07222-2 **PARISIAN NIGHTS #134** Susanna Collins $1.95
_____ 07233-0 **GOLDEN ILLUSIONS #135** Sarah Crewe $1.95
_____ 07224-9 **ENTWINED DESTINIES #136** Rachel Wayne $1.95
_____ 07225-7 **TEMPTATION'S KISS #137** Sandra Brown $1.95
_____ 07226-5 **SOUTHERN PLEASURES #138** Daisy Logan $1.95
_____ 07227-3 **FORBIDDEN MELODY #139** Nicola Andrews $1.95
_____ 07228-1 **INNOCENT SEDUCTION #140** Cally Hughes $1.95
_____ 07229-X **SEASON OF DESIRE #141** Jan Mathews $1.95
_____ 07230-3 **HEARTS DIVIDED #142** Francine Rivers $1.95
_____ 07231-1 **A SPLENDID OBSESSION #143** Francesca Sinclaire $1.95
_____ 07232-X **REACH FOR TOMORROW #144** Mary Haskell $1.95
_____ 07233-8 **CLAIMED BY RAPTURE #145** Marie Charles $1.95
_____ 07234-6 **A TASTE FOR LOVING #146** Frances Davies $1.95
_____ 07235-4 **PROUD POSSESSION #147** Jena Hunt $1.95
_____ 07236-2 **SILKEN TREMORS #148** Sybil LeGrand $1.95
_____ 07237-0 **A DARING PROPOSITION #149** Jeanne Grant $1.95
_____ 07238-9 **ISLAND FIRES #150** Jocelyn Day $1.95
_____ 07239-7 **MOONLIGHT ON THE BAY #151** Maggie Peck $1.95
_____ 07241-9 **INTIMATE SCOUNDRELS #153** Cathy Thacker $1.95

All of the above titles are $1.75 per copy except where noted

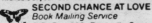
SK-41b

WHAT READERS SAY ABOUT
SECOND CHANCE AT LOVE BOOKS